DANGEROUS SURRENDER

THE SERAFINA: SIN CITY SERIES

Katie Reus

Copyright © 2014 by Katie Reus

All rights reserved. Except as permitted under the U.S. Copyright Act of 1976, no part of this publication may be reproduced, distributed, or transmitted in any form or by any means, or stored in a database or retrieval system, without the prior written permission of the author. Thank you for buying an authorized version of this book and complying with copyright laws. You're supporting writers and encouraging creativity.

Cover art: Jaycee of Sweet 'N Spicy Designs
JRT Editing
Author website: http://www.katiereus.com

Publisher's Note: This is a work of fiction. Names, characters, places, and incidents are either the products of the author's imagination or used fictitiously, and any resemblance to actual persons, living or dead, or business establishments, organizations or locales is completely coincidental.

Dangerous Surrender/Katie Reus. -- 1st ed.

ISBN-13: 978-1502561831
ISBN-10: 1502561832

eISBN: 9780996087483

For Kari Walker. Thank you, again, for always being in my corner.

Praise for the novels of Katie Reus

"…an engrossing page-turner that I enjoyed in one sitting. Reus offers all the ingredients I love in a paranormal romance." —Book Lovers, Inc.

"Has all the right ingredients: a hot couple, evil villains, and a killer action-filled plot. . . . [The] Moon Shifter series is what I call Grade-A entertainment!" —Joyfully Reviewed

"I could not put this book down. . . . Let me be clear that I am not saying that this was a good book *for* a paranormal genre; it was an excellent romance read, *period*." —All About Romance

"Reus strikes just the right balance of steamy sexual tension and nail-biting action….This romantic thriller reliably hits every note that fans of the genre will expect." —*Publisher's Weekly*

"Prepare yourself for the start of a great new series! . . . I'm excited about reading more about this great group of characters." —Fresh Fiction

"Nonstop action, a solid plot, good pacing and riveting suspense…" —*RT Book Reviews (4.5 Stars)*

"Wow! This powerful, passionate hero sizzles with sheer deliciousness. I loved every sexy twist of this fun & exhilarating tale. Katie Reus delivers!" —Carolyn Crane, author of *Into the Shadows*

Continued…

"You'll fall in love with Katie's heroes."
—*New York Times* bestselling author, Kaylea Cross

"A sexy, well-crafted paranormal romance that succeeds with smart characters and creative world building."—Kirkus Reviews

"*Mating Instinct*'s romance is taut and passionate . . . Katie Reus's newest installment in her Moon Shifter series will leave readers breathless!" —Stephanie Tyler, *New York Times* bestselling author

"Reus has definitely hit a home run with this series. . . . This book has mystery, suspense, and a heart-pounding romance that will leave you wanting more." —Nocturne Romance Reads

"Katie Reus pulls the reader into a story line of second chances, betrayal, and the truth about forgotten lives and hidden pasts."
—The Reading Café

"If you are looking for a really good, new military romance series, pick up *Targeted*! The new Deadly Ops series stands to be a passionate and action-riddled read."
—That's What I'm Talking About

"Sexy suspense at its finest."
—Laura Wright, *New York Times* bestselling author of *Branded*

CHAPTER ONE

Taylor Arenas smoothed a hand down her light-gray, pencil skirt as she exited the main elevator onto her boss's floor. Normally she just wore jeans and a casual top to work, but today she'd pulled out all the stops and actually gone for the business-professional look.

She resisted the urge to wipe her damp palm on her skirt as her heels clicked against the tiled entryway on the tenth floor. The ten-story building in Oceanside, California was non-descript on the outside so that most people didn't know what went on here.

Today she wondered if *she* even knew what Powers Group did. Or whether it was all one big lie.

The glass and metal desk the executive assistant sat behind wasn't occupied. No surprise since it was only six in the morning. Taylor was early for a reason. She needed to talk to Hugh Powers and couldn't wait a second longer. Since he was often in by five-thirty, she had no doubt he'd be here.

And with her all-access card to the building she was one of the few people who could get to this floor without bothering with security. Even if she didn't have the access card she could have just hacked her way in. Which was one of the reasons Hugh had hired her five years ago, fresh out of college. There were only three offices on this floor; two for the owners and one belonged to the head of security, Benjamin Escobar.

With her slim briefcase in one hand, she bypassed the first two and went straight to the last one at the end. This morning the glass walls of Hugh's office weren't frosted over and his door was propped open. But she easily saw he wasn't inside before she'd even neared the door.

As she stepped inside, the door to his private bathroom opened. Since it didn't have a regular door, it was as if the wall opened up. When it was closed it was difficult to see the seam.

His dark eyebrows rose as he looked at her attire. In his early fifties, he was a handsome, fit man graying at the temples with a sprinkling just starting to show throughout the rest of his hair. Even when he was dressed in board shorts ready to surf—

and that was as often as he could—he had a regal air about him. "Is there a meeting I forgot about?"

She shook her head.

"Good because I don't think those zombie shoes would cut it." His lips twitched at the corners.

Okay, maybe her heeled pumps weren't business-professional, not with the green and pink zombie teeth design covering the front and the skulls dotting the sides. But they made her feel better, more normal. She swallowed hard. "We need to talk." She hated that her voice came out shaky.

His dark blue eyes filled with concern, which made her angrier. If he was the liar he appeared to be, she didn't want his fake-caring. He pointed at one of the seats in front of his beat up desk. "Sit," he said quietly. The man could afford anything he wanted but he still had the piece of crap desk he'd gotten from a big, box store decades ago before he'd made his millions. She'd always thought that said so much about the type of man he was. He'd never forgotten how far he'd come.

She prayed she wasn't wrong about him. If he was ripping off his own company . . . it would break her heart.

Swallowing hard, she didn't bother taking off her coat as she sat ramrod straight and met his gaze.

"For the last week I've been working on investigating those six companies you wanted me to." She had a tendency to ramble when she was nervous so she cut right to the point. "Long explanation short, in the process of my investigation I ran across some files regarding Chemagan." She paused, waiting for a reaction, but Hugh just nodded, listening intently as he always did when she outlined something for him. He didn't seem disturbed at all by the mention of the company. "I visited the Chemagan building yesterday." A new company Powers Group had been funneling money into the past six months. A company that didn't actually exist.

He frowned. "You did?" He seemed genuinely confused.

For the first time in a week Taylor allowed a sliver of relief to slide through her veins. He didn't seem defensive or worried. She nodded and set her briefcase on the desk. She'd taken pictures of the decrepit building yesterday with her phone but had them blown up to 8x10s and printed. She pulled out a stack and slid them across the desk to him.

He looked down, scanned them, then looked back at her in confusion. "What is this?"

"Chemagan. A company you've been putting a lot of research and development funds into the past six months." Or someone was. She pulled out two pages of financials, a condensed version of the trail of money she'd discovered.

"What the hell?" he muttered, scanning the readout.

She could have emailed it to him, but she'd wanted to see him in person, to confront him and to see if he was a crook and a liar. Taylor didn't trust many people but Hugh had given her a job when she was twenty-two and in the last five years he'd become the only father figure she'd ever had. This kind of fraud could bring down his company, everything he'd worked for. And in her experience people weren't just a little dirty. That type of dirty business outlook expanded to all aspects of their lives, like a cancer. She just couldn't believe that he'd been hiding what type of man he was, that he'd somehow fooled everyone, including her.

"This is way too much R&D..." Trailing off, he glanced at the pictures again. He picked up one, his jaw clenching tight. "You're sure this is Chemagan?"

"You've never been there?"

He shook his head. "No, this is one of . . . Neal's projects."

Neal Lynch was Hugh's partner and a man Taylor tolerated because she had to. Ten years younger than Hugh, the two had partnered up over a decade ago, before Taylor had even known who Hugh Powers was.

To her surprise Hugh let out a savage curse. "Thank you for bringing this to my attention."

Taylor shifted slightly in her seat. "Everything is in your name, Hugh."

His jaw tightened again, the anger in his blue eyes palpable. "That bastard . . . All that R&D money has to be going somewhere. We need to find out where. It'll prove what he's been up to. Whatever the hell this is," he said, gesturing to the photos and paperwork on his desk.

Hugh seemed angry but not exactly surprised. "Hugh, has he done something like this before?"

Her boss shook his head. "Not that I know of, but lately . . . he's had some money problems the past year. His divorce and other personal stuff."

Personal meaning his gambling problem, something Taylor was aware of, but she didn't comment on directly. "Are you going to involve the authorities?"

He let out a long sigh and glanced back down at the readout. "Maybe. I need to figure out how deep this goes and who else is involved, then we'll have a better game plan. If it'll effect the company . . . honestly, I don't know that I'll prosecute, but if we can get enough leverage to oust him, he'll be done in business. I'll make sure of it."

She nodded, relief slamming through her now that she knew Hugh wasn't involved. Unless he was the best actor in the world, then she believed him. He'd never given her a reason not to and he was so successful that she couldn't imagine why he would start stealing from his own company. Neal, however, did. "I can help with that." Because she had no problem working to bring Neal down. In fact, she relished the idea. The guy was a creep on a personal level, but stealing from his own company and making it look like his partner did it? Super douche. "Do you mind if I use your bathroom?"

He shook his head and pressed a button under his desk. The door on the wall made a soft snicking sound as it opened a couple inches. Standing, she made her way to the plush room and pulled the door shut behind her. Her hands were still damp with sweat so she washed them, then splashed cold water on her cheeks. She'd been so consumed with worry that she hadn't been able to eat much for almost two days. The jittery effect was finally catching up to her.

As she turned from the sink back to the door, she shook her head at the sight of the panel of four video screens. Even in here Hugh had to be in control. She loved her boss but he was a bit of a freak when it came to security like this. He had a shot of his office, outside the main lobby, in the main lobby and a shot of the hallway outside his office.

She started to exit the bathroom when she saw Neal Lynch in the hallway heading for Hugh's office. *Ugh.* He came in early sometimes too and she really didn't want to see him now. She didn't think she'd be able to hide her disgust of him. When he appeared in the doorway to Hugh's office, Hugh started gathering the photographs.

There was no sound unfortunately so all she could see was their interactions and hear a muffled conversation. She hoped Hugh didn't give them away. She didn't want to give Neal time to start covering his tracks. Hugh took one of the photos and shoved it at Neal.

Uh oh.

"You fucking bastard!" Hugh's angry shout carried through the bathroom door.

Well so much for not giving them away. They needed time to gather evidence against Neal, not tip their hands. Too late for that now.

On screen Neal said something then Hugh shoved another photo at him, right into his chest. *Damn it, Hugh, what are you thinking?* Worry spiked inside her.

Neal said something else, still too low for Taylor to hear. He turned away, leaving, and Taylor breathed out a sigh of relief. They might just have to call the cops on him or at least have security escort him from the building. If they revoked all his access to the company system immediately then she'd be able to gather the evidence she needed, she was sure of it.

Suddenly he whirled back and pulled out a gun from the interior of his jacket. He aimed it at Hugh.

Pop, pop, pop.

Her boss stumbled backward, sprawling on the desk as blood bloomed on his chest.

Oh my god, oh my god, oh my god. Taylor slapped her hand over her mouth. She had to get help, to call someone to—oh my god! Neal stiffened as his gaze landed on her briefcase. He knew she was here.

Run.

His gaze swiveled toward the seamless entrance to the bathroom. With smooth movements he strode toward Hugh's desk.

Taylor hurried toward the other door that exited to the foyer for the executive elevator. Her heels clacked on the tile as she yanked it open. Panic slithered through her veins as she spilled out into the open room that led to Hugh's private elevator. When he'd bought this building he'd made a few modifications, the executive elevator being one of them.

Without glancing behind her she raced across the open space and punched in Hugh's code. Her fingers shook but she got it right the first time. The doors whooshed open and she dove inside, her heart slamming against her ribs double-time.

She hit her finger against the garage button then the button to close the doors. *Come on!*

The bathroom door opened, ricocheting loudly against the wall as Neal strode out. "You stupid bitch," he growled, raising his gun.

Taylor dove to the side, trying to hide as the doors started to close. The pinging of the bullets against the metal doors was like rain on a tin roof until the door finally whooshed shut in a rush.

Her heart hammered wildly in her chest as the elevator descended. Only as the door opened into the garage did she realize she'd been shot.

***

Neal cursed as the elevator slid closed behind that bitch Taylor. She was too fucking smart for her own good.

Think, think, think.

He'd only have minutes to act, minutes to get everything in order, to cover his tracks. He whipped out one of his cell phones as he backtracked to Hugh's private bathroom and through his office. Ignoring his dead partner's body, he dialed 9-1-1 as he hurried down the hallway.

"9-1-1 operator, what is your emergency?" a woman with a crisp, serious voice asked.

"My partner . . . he's dead. She shot him!" He sounded panicked even to himself as he reached his office. Immediately he started tugging his jacket and shirt off. He had to strip, shower in his private bathroom and scrub off all the gunshot residue from his hands and any on his body. He'd be disposing of his clothes and the gun, which wasn't registered to him. And he'd be pinning everything on her. If it was his word against hers he had no doubt the cops would believe him.

"Who's been shot, sir?"

"My partner, Hugh Powers. I came in to work early like I usually do and found Taylor Arenas in his office standing over his dead body with a gun in her hand. I barely managed to escape. She tried to shoot me too but I was able to make it to our executive elevator."

"Sir, I need your physical address."

After he rattled it off, he said, "I just left him lying there. I need to check on him."

"No, sir. If you're in a safe location you need to stay where you are. I've got officers and paramedics en route now."

"He's my partner, my mentor. I . . . I've gotta check on him. He could still be alive."

"Sir—"

He hung up on her. Later when questioned he'd say he lost service in the elevator, which he hadn't been in. But they'd never know that. He was going to turn the story around so that he was the victim and Taylor the aggressor.

Half-stripped, he sat in front of his computer and pulled up the security feeds. As a partner he had access to everything in the building. Not using his code, but Hugh's, he logged in and deleted today's and yesterday's feeds. Taylor had wanted to upgrade their system so that everything transmitted to an external server, but Hugh had shot her down because he wanted to keep his old-school technology. Very anti-Big Brother, he hadn't wanted outsiders to have access to anything to do with his company. Now the old man's stubbornness was going to let Neal get away with his murder. The irony made him smile.

Next he turned off the security feed completely. Taylor was a genius with computers so it made sense she'd be able to hack in and erase what she'd done. As soon as he was done deleting the files, he tugged off his pants and balled all his clothes together, hurrying back toward his private bathroom.

Shaking, he scrubbed himself raw from head to foot, taking care with his hands and face, the places that had been exposed. He read enough and watched enough television that he knew gunshot residue washed away easily enough. Getting rid of his clothes would be important though. He couldn't do it now, but he would soon enough. Until then he'd have to stash them . . . Where?

There was an empty conference room on the floor below. He could stash it up above one of the ceiling tiles. That would work, especially since the security cameras were off.

What else . . . shit, he had to make sure there wasn't any blood in the elevator she'd escaped in. He didn't think he'd hit her, but if he had, he needed to wipe up the evidence.

Hurrying out of his bathroom, he was relieved to find his office still empty. The head of security wouldn't be in for another hour but he'd need to call him. First, he had another call to make. He grabbed one of his burner cell phones from a hidden compartment in his desk drawer. He glanced at the clock on his wall. He had maybe seven minutes left. At least it would take the police a few minutes to get upstairs once they made it to the building.

His contact picked up on the second ring. "Yeah?"

"Taylor Arenas is on her way to the police station. I need her to disappear quietly. It needs to look like she's gone on the run. Ten thousand in your bank account today if you do it." He was going to make sure that she died one way or another. Even if she went to the police, they'd believe him over her. They'd have to. And he'd make sure she 'killed herself' over her guilt from taking Hugh's life. He just hoped it didn't come to that. It'd be much easier if she simply disappeared.

"I'm on my way. What happens if I can't get to her in time?"

"Make sure that you do." Otherwise he was screwed. "Call me when it's done." He hung up and turned off the phone before tucking it into the bundle of clothes. He wouldn't be using it again and would dispose of it along with his gun and clothes. Next he hurriedly got dressed in a spare set of clothes he kept at the office before grabbing Lysol wipes from the bathroom. If there was blood in the elevator he'd clean it. After that he'd call his head of security then go back to Hugh's office. He needed to bend down near the body and act as if he'd given Hugh CPR, make sure the evidence proved that he was telling the truth.

Once he checked the elevator and found no blood, the weight on his shoulders lifted. If she hadn't been shot, that made all this easier. It was a classic he-said, she-said situation. He had another throwaway gun he'd planned to leave next to Hugh's body to make it look as if Hugh had shot Taylor if need be. But it didn't look like that would be necessary.

Dragging in a deep breath, he realized he could still get away with this. He just needed to remain focused and make sure Taylor Arenas disappeared for good.

CHAPTER TWO

Discomfort slid through Taylor's side when she shifted slightly against the driver's seat of Hugh's vehicle. She thought she'd been shot a lot worse but now realized it was barely a graze. A strip of skin had been ripped away, but she was barely bleeding.

Not that she even cared. She just wanted to get the hell away from work and tell the police. She didn't have any of her personal belongings with her, like her cell phone. No, unfortunately that was in her car. In the company parking garage. She'd been so damn terrified that Neal would catch up to her that she'd taken Hugh's SUV since it had been right there when she'd exited the garage.

Programmed with fingerprint software, she'd been able to start it with her thumb print since he'd given her access to all his vehicles. She'd been driving for a couple minutes, but her hands were still shaky and her breathing choppy. Even though she had no control of it, she knew she was in a state of mild shock. She also knew that she had to call the police. She was only a few minutes away from the station anyway, but they needed to catch Neal before he escaped.

With a trembling hand, she pressed the OnStar call button on the rearview mirror. As soon as she told the system to call 9-1-1, some of her panic started to ebb.

She might not trust the police, but in a situation like this she knew they would help. Her mentor had been gunned down right in front of her and that bastard Neal was going to pay for what he'd done. Anger and grief battled inside her, each one wanting dominance. She let her rage take control, needing that emotion in charge because once she let herself grieve, she knew she'd be a useless wreck.

As soon as the 9-1-1 operator answered, asking what her emergency was, Taylor found her voice. "My boss has been shot. Killed. I just saw Neal Lynch murder Hugh Powers!" She didn't mean to shout, but felt out of control, her entire body still shaking. She gave the address, her heart an erratic drumbeat in her chest. It was hard to breathe past the pain as she thought of Hugh slumping back against his desk, blood pooling everywhere.

"Take a deep breath ma'am. Who am I speaking to?"

"Taylor Arenas. I work at Powers Group."

There was a slight pause. "What's the name of the man you saw shot?"

"Hugh Powers. He's in his office, on the top floor of the Powers Group building. That bastard Neal Lynch just shot him in cold blood." Her stomach lurched as she remembered everything in vivid, Technicolor detail.

"Where are you now ma'am?"

"I'm on my way to the police station."

"Why don't you pull over and I'll have an officer meet you?" The woman's voice was calm, and she was sure the woman meant to be reassuring, but something about her tone rubbed Taylor the wrong way. She knew she was just being paranoid though. The woman only wanted to help.

"No, I'll be there in like, two minutes. Look, who cares about an officer meeting me? Send someone to the Powers Group before Neal gets away!"

"Ma'am, we already have officers there. I need you to tell me exactly where you are." Now her voice was forceful, demanding.

What the hell? Alarm bells dinged in Taylor's head. She knew she was likely being paranoid but . . . She pressed the end button on the phone call. Why were officers already at the building? Someone would have had to call. And the building had been empty except for . . . Neal. Had he called? But why would he call for a crime he'd committed? Unless he was telling the cops she did it.

She shook her head. No, the evidence wouldn't lie.

Frowning, she turned left into the parking lot of the local police station. Palm trees waved beautifully under the clear, blue sky. There should be dark, stormy clouds filling the sky, not beauty on a day like this. On a day one of the most important people in her life had died. Tears stung her eyes, but she blinked them back.

She'd break down later. First she needed to talk to the police. The phone rang on the vehicle system, but she ignored it. Driving around the parking lot, she started to park in a spot on the front row but nearly crashed when she saw Gordon Simpson hovering near the front entrance. Wearing black pants and a long, black, dress shirt, he was smoking a cigarette and glancing around. Was he looking for her? If he was he'd probably be looking for her car. Unless he knew she'd taken Hugh's vehicle . . . adrenaline punched through her as she gripped the wheel even tighter.

Simpson was part of the security team for the Powers Group and he sometimes worked closely with Neal. What was he doing here? Her heart rate kicked up a notch when he nodded at a man in a suit entering the building. The other man's badge was clearly visible so he was a cop. Maybe a detective, given the attire. Had Neal sent Simpson here for her? That seemed so insane but she never would have imagined that Neal would shoot Hugh in cold blood, either.

Shifting against the seat, she took her pea coat off, groaning at the discomfort. There was a tear in her coat and her bloody blouse. Crimson stained the pale pink material. She ripped the side of her shirt open a little more to eye the wound fully. A strip of skin was gone, blood trickled down her side, and a dull throb pulsed from the gash. The bullet had literally skimmed her body.

She looked back up and saw Simpson still talking to the cop, laughing at something the man said. Making a split-second decision, she looked in the rearview mirror and reversed. She needed to get home, get the safe deposit key to her bank and retrieve the evidence she'd found regarding the Chemagan company. She'd show it to the police and explain everything that had happened this morning.

Her stepfather had been a cop—an asshole who'd used to shove her mother around until he'd finally killed her in a drunken rage—and Taylor knew how the system worked. Her mom had been murdered because of a department that looked the other way. Once she'd died they'd been all apologetic and talked about how no one had seen the signs, blah, blah blah. When she came to the police she needed irrefutable proof, especially since she wouldn't put it above Neal to try and twist this whole situation, to frame her. He'd probably claim he shot her in self-defense. And it was clear he had contacts in the department. It turned her stomach.

By the time she made it to her condo complex, the adrenaline rush from earlier was fading. Her hands were clammy and her body was numb as she pulled into the parking lot. When she saw two uniformed police officers standing guard at the entrance, another spike of fear jagged through her like lightning. She kept driving as if she was looking for a parking spot and exited out another entrance.

In the five years since she'd lived here she'd never seen the police here once. No, they had to be here for her.

Which meant Neal had done something to set her up. No way was she getting arrested and railroaded. Shit, she needed to think, to clear her head and come up with a game plan. And she couldn't do that here in Oceanside. She needed outside help. There weren't many people she trusted, but her friend Vadim Sokolov in Vegas would be able to. And the drive wasn't too far.

She turned onto the street and headed away from her building. As soon as she ditched Hugh's SUV and found another vehicle, she'd be on her way. At least Hugh had a couple hundred bucks in his center console or she'd be totally screwed. It was good she didn't have a phone though. No way to trace her.

***

Almost six hours later Taylor pulled up to Vadim's house, dust from the long, dirt road behind her kicking up. He lived out in the desert, a good distance from any neighbors. The man was a loner. Or had been until recently when he'd gotten married. She'd hated that she hadn't been able to make it to the wedding but at least she'd gotten to meet his new wife, a sweet, adorable woman aptly named Angel.

She tried calling Vadim again from one of the burner phones she'd picked up at a Podunk gas station but it went to his voicemail. Again.

Damn it.

She parked in his driveway and turned off the engine. She'd ended up stealing a beat up, pale blue Pinto. The radio had been sketchy and the passenger door had spots that were almost rusted all the way through, but the engine had been good enough to make the drive to Vegas so she had no complaints. Even if someone reported it stolen—and the owner was probably secretly thanking her for taking it—there was no way to track it electronically.

She'd almost kept Hugh's SUV because he'd disabled his GPS tracking. The man was—had been—paranoid of too much government power and the ability of so many, not just the government, to track others' whereabouts. He'd disabled the GPS tracking in anything, even his phone. But in her shock-filled haze she'd remembered that she could be tracked through the OnStar system regardless of what Hugh had done.

God, she missed him and his quirkiness. A fresh wave of pain swept through her and her throat tightened as she opened the driver's side door, but she refused to cry. Not yet. Not until she had help and a game plan.

On the drive from Oceanside to Vegas she'd stopped twice; for gas and to get supplies which included a first aid kit, burner phones, and new clothes. Considering her current attire was from the first gas station/truck stop she'd stopped at, she looked ridiculous wearing a Golden State T-shirt snagged from the teenage boys' section. The sweatpants with the word California down the outside of both legs were actually made for women, but they'd only had them in long sizes so she'd rolled them up at the ankles. With her zombie heels she looked as if she was doing the walk of shame.

Whatever, she was alive. The bandage she'd put on over her wound was holding and the ibuprofen she'd taken had helped with her headache and lessened the throb in her wound. Unfortunately she was exhausted and running on fumes. She'd been so eaten up with worry the last few days she hadn't slept at all. Combined with the shock of seeing her friend killed and being shot herself, she was about to pass out.

Not to mention the freaking cops wanted her for questioning. She'd called two friends from work on the way to Vegas and each of them had said the police wanted to talk to her. One had even asked if she'd killed Hugh. Fucker. She'd used one of her burner phones to call both friends before ditching the phone. And she'd called while she'd still been in Oceanside. So if the cops somehow triangulated where she'd been calling from, they'd have no leads. She wouldn't be taking any more chances now by calling anyone because she had a feeling they'd be ready to track her.

Besides, she already knew what she needed to. Neal had somehow set her up. She couldn't figure out how he could have changed the evidence, but she couldn't think very clearly about anything right now.

After knocking on the front door and ringing the bell with no answer, she had the childish urge to stomp her feet. But she'd come this far. She wasn't turning around now. And the truth was, she felt safe here.

She tried pulling up the garage door up by hand, but it didn't budge. No surprise. Fortunately for her, she knew how to release the safety latch. It was completely criminal but right about now she was thankful for her less than savory skills.

Returning to the Pinto, she drove it right up until it was almost touching the garage door. Then she unbent the metal hanger she'd gotten with the T-shirt she was wearing. She was just glad she hadn't tossed the thing. Climbing onto the hood, she slid her hand through the top part of the garage, breaking a nail as she pulled the vinyl material down as much as she could. Not much, but there wasn't a foamy seal in place so she was able to slip the thin hanger through. Later she'd yell at Vadim for this lapse in security.

Sliding the hanger around, she wiggled it until it caught on something. On her second try, she felt and heard the latch pull free.

Bingo.

Once upon a time it would have taken her exactly six seconds to do this. Now, it took her fifteen. Not bad.

After reversing the car away from the garage door, she tested it again and breathed out in relief when it slid upward. Leaving the door halfway open, she grabbed her two plastic bags from the vehicle. One held her bloody clothes and the other all the stuff she'd gotten at the two gas stations.

The lock on the interior door was decent, but she picked it. As soon as she stepped from the garage into the utility room the alarm started beeping. She wavered on her feet, but the beeping sound spurred her into action. She had fifteen to thirty seconds to disarm it.

On the third try she got it right. The code was the day, month and year Vadim had gotten his dog Charlie. Not something most people would know, but she and Vadim went way back. She'd apologize later and yell at him for the code too.

Of course he'd probably yell at her for breaking into his house but she was doing him a favor by pointing out his security flaws. She snorted at herself as she opened the utility room door into his kitchen.

Fully expecting to find Charlie bounding toward her, she frowned at the silence. That was when it hit her. When she'd been ringing the bell and knocking on the door there had been no scuffling inside from the dog. Nothing.

Charlie was almost always here unless Vadim took her to work. "Hello?" Taylor called out, her voice cracking from sheer exhaustion.

No response. She tried calling Vadim again on her burner phone as she stepped farther into the kitchen. She slipped her heels off and froze when she saw a pile of about a dozen gifts on the small table by one of the windows.

Holy shit, Vadim and Angel were still on their honeymoon. No wonder he wasn't answering his phone. Taylor vaguely remembered him telling her they'd be going away for three weeks. Bora Bora or somewhere.

Iciness flooded her as the last of her energy faded from her body. She'd been banking on Vadim's help. She blinked rapidly, trying to shake off the new wave of exhaustion and despair threatening to pull her under, the invisible sandbags weighing her eyelids down, making her want to fall asleep right on the kitchen floor.

Bags in hand, she stumbled toward the nearest guest bathroom. She needed to change her bandage and maybe close her eyes for a few minutes. And . . . she grabbed a bottle of vodka from the pantry on the way. She didn't know what kind of first aid stuff he had and vodka would kill anything.

And she really wanted a swig because right about now, she knew she was in deep shit.

CHAPTER THREE

Roman scanned Vadim's property as he pulled up behind an unfamiliar Pinto with a California plate. Frowning, he snapped a picture of the license plate before getting out of his truck. Vadim lived on the outskirts of town with no neighbors for miles. That car had definitely seen better days. Other than the unfamiliar vehicle, everything else looked normal. Just wide-open desert for miles around greeted him. There was no way in hell someone had accidentally stumbled on his place.

No one was supposed to be here. Hell, he hadn't even planned on coming by. He'd just wanted to get one of Charlie's favorite chew toys he'd forgotten the other day. He'd brought her by Vadim and Angel's place a couple days ago because 'Angel' was worried about Charlie getting homesick while she and Vadim were on their honeymoon. In reality, Roman knew it was Vadim worried about the mutt. For such a hard ass, V had two soft spots: Angel and Charlie the German shepherd.

Withdrawing his weapon, Roman felt the hood of the Pinto with his free hand. The engine was cool. He ducked down and glanced under the partially open garage door to look inside.

No one was there and Vadim's Mercedes S-Class sat untouched. Roman crawled under, not disturbing the position of the door before heading to the interior door. If someone had broken in, he'd have them arrested.

Weapon out, he slowly turned the handle then nudged it open with his foot. The door chime dinged, announcing that someone was entering the house, but the alarm didn't go off, making him tense. Disabling Vadim's system would take skill unless someone had the security code. The utility room was also empty. Moving on silent feet, he swept through the kitchen.

A pair of high heels with . . . zombies on them sat haphazardly next to one of the island chairs in the otherwise pristine kitchen. A woman had broken in? Some gifts from the recent wedding were still unopened too. Vadim and Angel had left so quickly after their ceremony they hadn't been able to open the gifts people had brought to the wedding.

Pausing, Roman listened intently. It sounded like running water coming from one of the bathrooms. He'd been in Vadim's home on multiple occasions, especially back when he'd been giving Angel self-defense lessons. There were three bedrooms on the east side with the living room connecting the kitchen, dining room and library. Vadim's office was connected off the living room, more or less a separate entity from the rest of the house.

The water had to be coming from one of the bathrooms. Since Vadim had good insulation in this place, Roman guessed it was the nearest one. Moving quickly but quietly, he made his way through the kitchen, then the living room, wondering how the hell someone got past Vadim's security system.

As he neared the closest bedroom the sound grew louder. Bypassing it, he swept the rest of the house to find it clear before returning to the first guestroom.

The door was ajar so he slipped inside without having to move it. Empty.

His breathing and heart rate were steady. If an intruder thought they could fuck with his friends' home while they were gone, they were in for a surprise. For a brief moment he contemplated calling the cops, but he was a former Marine and now personal security for one of the wealthiest men in the world. If he couldn't handle one intruder, he needed a new fucking job.

Steam billowed out from the open bathroom door, but he didn't hear the kind of change in the water's rhythm that went along with someone showering. He frowned and gently pushed the door open.

All stone and tile that looked like sandstone, there were sparkly pieces of glass on the wall that made up the shower enclosure. The room seemed to shimmer. A shadow was behind the enclosure, but it was unmoving.

Stepping to the side, he brought his weapon fully up and swept around the shower entrance to find a naked woman slumped on the built-in bench, a bottle of vodka grasped loosely in one hand as blood trickled down her side. Long, dark hair was plastered around her face and over her shoulders and breasts.

Shit.

This could be some sort of trap but he doubted it. Holstering his weapon, he stepped inside the enclosure, ignoring the pulsing jets and water splashing him as he twisted the shower knob off.

Crouching in front of her, he felt the pulse point at her throat.

Steady.

Leaning down, he inspected the open wound along the woman's ribcage. If he wasn't mistaken, that was a—the woman shifted suddenly.

Screaming, she swung the vodka bottle at him. Roman ducked and grabbed her wrist, yanking it downward. She released the bottle. It crashed to the tile floor, glass shattering.

"Don't fucking touch me!" the woman screamed, trying to wiggle away from him as he hoisted her off the bench, holding her around the waist—and tried to ignore how soft her lush body felt against his. He tried to be careful with her wound but was more concerned with subduing her so she didn't hurt herself.

"Damn it, stop!" he ordered as she swung a fist at his head. He had one arm wrapped around her waist, holding her close and pinning one arm to her side, but she was moving around like an eel. "You're going to cut yourself if I drop you."

At that, she stilled. Breathing hard, she looked up at him. "You care if I cut my feet?"

He blinked once, mesmerized for a moment by the shocking blue of her eyes against her beautiful, almost caramel skin tone. Her eyes were like the Mediterranean on a clear day. "It's not like I want you to slice yourself up." What was the matter with her? And who the hell was she?

"Oh. Okay." She was still tense, her body coiled like a snake, waiting to strike, but she didn't try to punch him in the head again. Instead she held onto his shoulders and went semi-lax against him.

"I'm going to step out of the shower and put you on your feet. Okay?"

She nodded, her expression wary. Her eyes were wide and her teeth chattering, though she tried to hide it as she clenched her jaw tight.

His boots crunched over glass as he carefully moved backward. He didn't stop until they were on the tile of the bathroom and far away from the glass. "I'm going to put you down, but if you attack me, I will restrain your hands behind your back." He still might restrain her if it turned out she was a thief.

She swallowed hard, fear flickering in her gaze. Damn, he hated the sight of any woman being afraid of him, but he wasn't stupid enough to think women couldn't be dangerous. Just because she was petite and so fucking gorgeous it almost hurt to look at her, didn't mean he'd be letting his guard down around her. "I won't attack you."

As he placed her on her feet, he tried not to look but damn, his gaze dipped down to her breasts. Lush, full, a little more than a handful, he wondered what it'd be like to cup them…

"Pervert," she snapped, wrapping an arm around her chest before turning and grabbing a fluffy, white towel from one of the nearby racks.

She quickly wrapped it around herself but not before he got a full view of her entire, delectable body. She was petite with toned legs, but not lean. She was soft and curvy and he liked the little triangle of hair covering her mound. He supposed he could have pretended not to look, but why bother. He shrugged. "You're the one naked in my friend's house. Now why the hell are you here, passed out and wounded? Who are you?" He wanted to talk about the wound he'd seen on her ribcage. It was difficult to tell, but it might be a bullet ricochet.

Her eyes widened a fraction. "You're friends with Vadim?"

Surprised she knew his friend's name, Roman nodded. "Yeah. How do you know him?"

She pursed her lips together, eyeing him as if she didn't trust him—when she was the one who'd broken into Vadim's house.

"You know what, I'm calling the cops." He went to grab his cell phone from his back pocket but she held her hands up.

"No, wait! Vadim and I have been friends for years. We did some work together years ago, before he got out of . . . the military."

Roman lifted an eyebrow. "Which branch?"

She watched him for a long moment, clear she didn't trust him. Well the feeling was fucking mutual. Finally she said, "Marines."

He nodded. "That's right."

The tension in her shoulders seemed to relax at that. "The company I work for handled a couple government contracts and Vadim and I ended up working together. I came to see him because . . . well, it doesn't matter. I forgot he'd still be on his honeymoon or I'd have never come. If you'll just let me get dressed I'll be on my way. No harm, right?" She laughed nervously and he didn't miss the little wince she tried to cover up.

He frowned, ignoring the last part of what she'd said. He could see a spot of blood coming through the towel where she'd been wounded. "What kind of trouble are you in? Did someone fucking shoot you?"

Her beautiful face paled. "No."

His jaw tightened. "Don't lie to me."

When she didn't respond he sighed and pulled his cell phone out.

"Wait—"

"I'm not calling the cops," he muttered. "What's your name?" he demanded as he scrolled to Angel's number.

He raised his eyebrows when she didn't respond, watching and waiting. Finally she sighed, seeming almost defeated. "Taylor."

Though Roman hated to interrupt Vadim and Angel, this called for it.

Vadim answered the phone on the second ring. "Why the hell are you calling my wife on our honeymoon?" he growled, not much heat behind his voice. "Is everything okay with Charlie?"

"Your dog is fine. There's a woman at your house who says she knows you. Broke in, but hasn't touched anything. She passed out in the shower and I'm pretty sure she's been shot."

"Are you fucking with me?"

"Nope. Says her name is Taylor. Dark hair, blue eyes, not very tall." He wasn't sure he bought her story.

The woman just wrapped her arms tighter around her middle, looking young and vulnerable; the sight disturbing to Roman.

"Taylor Arenas?" Vadim's voice was shocked.

"What's your last name?" Roman asked her.

She paused for a moment. "Arenas."

"Yep."

"Put me on speaker," Vadim demanded.

"Hold on." Roman looked at Taylor as he held the phone out. "I'm putting Vadim on speaker."

The tension lines around her mouth lessened. "Okay."

"You're on," Roman said.

"Taylor? What's going on?" Vadim demanded.

"I . . . I'm in trouble, but I forgot you were on your honeymoon. I'm so sorry, Vadim. I never would have come here otherwise."

"Fuck that. What's going on?"

"Vadim, I . . . can we have some privacy?" she asked Vadim, carefully avoiding Roman's gaze as she stared at the phone.

Roman snorted as Vadim said, "Taylor, you can say anything in front of Roman. Anything. He's a former Marine too. I trust him with my life."

Well, damn.

She took a deep breath, her eyes filling up with tears, which she angrily swatted away. It was clear she didn't want Roman around but that was just too damn bad. "Long story short, Neal shot Hugh. He's been diverting funds to a bogus company and when Hugh confronted him, Neal just shot and killed him. I saw it happen and managed to escape—though he nicked me, but it's just a flesh wound. But now something else is going on. I think Neal is somehow framing me but I don't know how he'd have been able to do that. I guess he could have erased the video feeds at work but . . . I just don't know. When I went to the police station one of the security guys who works for Neal was waiting and then there were cops at my place when I went home. I called some people from work and they both told me the police want me for questioning. It sounded like they thought I killed Hugh so I just ran. I knew I needed to get out of the city and you were the first person I thought of."

Roman had no idea who the woman was talking about, but the way she spoke about them, without using last names, told him that Vadim must know the men. Or know of them.

"That motherfucker," Vadim growled. He took a deep breath. "You can't just run from the cops. You've been shot and you need to document it. You were shot at work?"

"Yeah."

"Where in the building were you shot?"

"Hugh's private elevator." She wrapped her arms tighter around her small frame and Roman found himself wanting to pull her into his arms.

After hearing her story it was clear someone needed to protect her. She sniffled once, looking even more lost.

"Okay. Go to the hospital now."

"I can't."

"You can and you will. Roman is going to take you and he's going to call a detective friend of ours."

Roman nodded. If Vadim trusted her and wanted to help her, he was going to trust her. He'd be doing some investigation of his own, but Vadim trusted almost no one. "Hurley?" he asked Vadim.

"Yes."

Taylor shook her head. "Vadim—"

"No. Listen to me. You need to get ahead of this now. Without knowing any more details, I know that running from the police makes you look guilty as shit. You have got to get in front of this. This all happened this morning?"

"Yeah." Her voice sounded small, broken.

Hell, if she'd just seen someone close to her get killed this morning Roman was impressed she was keeping it together.

"You can explain away your running through shock and fear, especially since you were shot and saw your boss killed. You've got to trust me on this. Roman will call Detective Hurley and have him meet you guys at the hospital. Roman?"

"I'm on it, man. Anything you need." He wasn't positive he trusted this woman, but he trusted Vadim. "Vadim, give me a second." He looked at Taylor and pointed to the door. "I'll be right outside." Without waiting for a response, he left the room and closed the door behind him

Taking it off speaker, he spoke quietly to his friend. "You sure you trust this woman?"

"Yes. Hugh Powers owns, or owned, Powers Group. He was like a father to Taylor. She never would have killed him. I'd stake everything I own on it. Neal Lynch is a sleazy bastard. I only met him once and it was enough for me. I believe in Taylor."

"Good enough for me."

"Thank you. I . . . owe you for this." Vadim had loosened up a little since he'd been with Angel, but that stiff, almost formalness crept back into his voice.

"You owe me for a shitload of stuff, including watching Charlie, and you know I'm going to collect." He kept his voice light.

Vadim just snorted and asked him to return to the bathroom so he could talk to Taylor. Vadim and Taylor talked for a few minutes until finally Vadim convinced her to listen to reason. He also read her the riot act for breaking into his place but Roman was pretty certain his friend was impressed she'd broken in. Roman certainly was. Once they were done talking, Roman promised to call Vadim with any updates before disconnecting.

"Why are you helping me?" she asked as Roman slid the phone back in his pocket.

"Because you're friends with Vadim and you clearly need it." He needed more information on her story, but if she was willing to meet with a detective, that went a long way in proving her innocence. Not to mention Vadim trusted her.

Her eyes welled with unexpected tears and to his surprise and horror, she started crying. Big, ugly tears. *Shit, shit, shit.* "Don't cry," he commanded, as if the order would somehow make her stop.

She sobbed out something that sounded a lot like, 'I don't know what's wrong with me' before she cupped her face in her hands.

Her shoulders shook as she tried to hold back her tears but he couldn't stand it anymore. Covering the short distance between them, he pulled her into his arms, rubbing a comforting hand down her spine. She buried her face against his chest and, taking him by surprise again, wrapped her arms around his waist and held on for dear life.

She might not know what was wrong with her, but he did. She'd seen someone close to her killed, she'd been shot and she was trying to deal with a shitty situation alone. On top of all that she was probably dealing with a healthy dose of shock and grief.

Even though Roman prided himself on staying away from any drama—unlike his twin—there was no way in hell he was walking away from a woman in need. After his father died, his mom had been left raising two, demanding boys. Looking back he knew how hard it had been on her. Maybe that was why something about women in need always called to him.

Even if he wasn't sure Taylor was innocent in all this, he'd be damned if he let her walk away with no protection.

CHAPTER FOUR

Neal glanced at Benjamin Escobar, the head of security for the Powers Group, as the man swiped his security card over the elevator pad. "You don't need to come with me."

Over six hours later, Neal had finally been allowed to return to the building now that Hugh's body had been removed and Neal had been processed for gunshot residue. He had some on him, which was easily explainable since he'd been in the vicinity of Taylor when she'd allegedly shot at him and because he'd supposedly gone to the aid of Hugh. It would be strange if he didn't have any on him, but there wasn't a ton of blowback on his current clothing, which was good. Now he needed to get rid of the other clothes and weapon he'd stashed and he couldn't do it with Escobar hanging around like his shadow.

Escobar, who was about the same height as him at five-ten, shot him a stony glance before motioning to the elevator door that opened. There was an intimidating air about him that Neal could never ignore. "I'm not leaving your side while you're here."

For some reason, Neal wasn't sure if Escobar was shadowing him because he was concerned, or for other reasons. He couldn't help but feel paranoid, especially after he'd killed Hugh, but Neal wondered if Escobar had somehow guessed. The man was a straight arrow and it was damn annoying. No, Neal was just being paranoid. How could Escobar have any clue?

"The security cameras are up and running again so you have nothing to worry about." Much to his annoyance the police had wanted to look at the video feeds immediately. He'd expected *that*. What he hadn't expected was for Escobar to be able to link everything back online so quickly, but he'd done it as soon as he'd arrived at the office that morning. Neal thought he'd knocked the system offline for a while. He knew he'd erased everything, but still . . . it made him edgy worrying about the clothes in the empty conference room.

"Hmm," was all Escobar said. Then, "Did Taylor say anything after shooting Hugh?"

Neal shook his head. "No. It all happened so fast. I guess she might have said something, but I was just trying to run for my life. It was . . . crazy. I still can't believe she killed him."

"Me either." As usual, Escobar's tone was unreadable.

Since Escobar clearly wasn't going to leave and Neal couldn't afford to make him suspicious, he decided to make use of him. "Will you bring Paige and Marissa up to my office? I want to speak to them."

Taylor had called Paige and Marissa after she'd gone on the run. He was still raging that his man hadn't been able to track down Taylor, but her running made her look guilty, which was damn good to solidify his story to the police. He wanted her dead though. Dead and gone so she couldn't cause him any trouble. And he still wasn't positive he hadn't shot her.

The police had examined the elevator and taken the bullets out of the outside of the doors, but they'd asked him a couple times if he'd been injured, wanting to take him down to the hospital. That line of questioning made him nervous. He hadn't seen any blood or bullet destruction in the elevator, but maybe he'd missed something.

Escobar nodded without looking at him as they reached the top floor. "Of course. I'll get them right now. What should I tell everyone else in the building?" He pressed the button to keep the door open as Neal stepped out.

Neal knew that almost everyone had stayed after he and Escobar had gone down to the police station. The crime scene and their floor was cordoned off from everyone and no one was actually working, but he guessed they didn't want to just leave either. "Everyone can go home. I'll let you handle making the announcement. I just..." He looked down, shaking his head as he covered his face with his hand, as if everything was too much for him to handle. "I can't deal with everyone right now." Taking a deep breath, he looked back up at the other man. "Tell everyone to come in tomorrow at ten. I'll set something up in the lobby and speak to everyone at the same time."

Escobar nodded and removed his hand from the elevator button, letting the doors close.

One of the first things Neal was going to do was fire that self-righteous bastard. But not right away. No, he needed to wait a couple months, to let everything die down before he made changes. For right now he couldn't afford any extra scrutiny.

He owed some terrifying people money, but he'd been making his payments. The last six months he'd had no problem covering his debt. The interest was what was killing him, but the Chemagan deal he'd set up had been brilliant. In another three months he'd planned to close it down and call it a loss with no one being the wiser, but that fucking bitch Taylor had somehow figured out what he was doing.

If his guy couldn't catch her before she resurfaced he had a plan to run if the cops believed her. He didn't think they would, but he was always prepared for a worst case scenario. Especially since he owed the Russian mob a shitload of money.

As he stepped into the hallway of the executive offices, he nodded once at the patrolman standing guard outside Hugh's office. They'd secured the area with tape and even though he'd told them that he would cut off access to this floor for everyone else, the police must have decided to leave a guard. The thought made him frown, but he shoved his unease aside and hurried to his own office.

After shutting the door behind him, he rummaged in his desk for another burner phone and called his contact with a trembling hand. It'd been fucking hours since he'd been able to make contact and it was making him edgy.

He picked up on the first ring. "Hey, boss."

"Tell me you have good news." His office was secure, with good insulation. There was no way the cop down the hall could hear him and no one else was currently on this floor. It was the only reason he was talking to his contact.

"Maybe. I called in a favor to one of my buddies at the PD. Narrowed down the reports of all the stolen vehicles around the time the target disappeared—"

"Get to the point," he snarled. His contact loved over-explaining what he did for Neal. He knew the guy was smart; it was why he used him. He didn't need a play-by-play.

There was a short pause, then he spoke with what sounded like gritted teeth. "There was a Pinto taken within a two block radius of where Hugh's SUV was found. I'm just surprised the owner reported it stolen. Anyway, the car blew through a few tolls. I know because . . . never mind. I can't know for certain but from the direction the car was going when it was pinged, compared against the addresses in her online address book, there's a possibility she's going to Vegas. She's got one contact in Vegas and I remember her talking about missing a wedding there a few weeks ago because of that business trip."

"Head there now." Taylor was smart and if she was running, she'd want to get some distance, but wouldn't want to go too far. Because Taylor wouldn't want to let Neal get away with hurting her precious mentor. And she wouldn't go to a hotel or motel because she was too smart to use her credit cards. No, she'd want to go to ground somewhere she felt safe.

"Hadn't heard from you so I'm already on my way. Should be at the address in half an hour."

"Who's the friend?"

"It just says Vadim S in her company address book. It's synced to her phone." He sounded smug but Neal was the one who'd given him access to her employee files so it wasn't as if he'd hacked into it.

The name Vadim was familiar, but Neal couldn't place it. Had the man done work for the company before? He frowned, wracking his brain, but shelved the name momentarily as he said, "Use any force necessary."

"What if she's got back up?"

"Everyone is expendable. If you have to do extra work, there's a bonus in it for you." He hated that he might have to pay his contact extra, especially when he needed all funds to go to the Russians or to his getaway stash. At least without Hugh around he wouldn't have to worry about hiding his diverted funds. For a while at least he could siphon off larger amounts, maybe completely pay off the Russians now instead of using his payment plan.

"Done. Going dark until I know if the target bolted here."

"Good. Don't fuck this up." He disconnected before his contact could respond. Perfect timing too. Escobar knocked even though he could see him clearly through the glass door of his office.

Neal stood and motioned for Escobar and the two women to enter. They both looked nervous, but that was to be expected. He rarely talked to them because he had no reason to. They were in IT and he had limited communication with them.

Pasting on what he hoped was an open, yet sad expression, he half-smiled at the women and motioned for them to sit in the seats in front of his desk. It was game time. He needed to know what Taylor had said to them. Even the smallest detail might give her away and he was determined to find her location at all costs.

* * *

Taylor looked up at the tall, incredibly sexy man she'd just sobbed all over like a complete maniac. He didn't seem too bothered by it, but she couldn't fight her embarrassment. She shouldn't even care, not after everything she'd been through today, but the man with mismatched eyes looked at her as if he could see every single thought she had. One eye was brown and the other a bluish-green, the unique combination making her feel even more off-kilter.

When she'd woken up with him crouching over her in the shower she'd completely lost it. Panic still hummed through her, that adrenaline blast in her system having barely faded at all. She cleared her throat. "I'm sorry for trying to hit you with a vodka bottle."

To her surprise, his lips curved up the tiniest fraction. She wondered if it was his version of a smile. "I need to look at your wound before we head to the hospital. At least put a bandage over it so you don't bleed through your clothes."

She looked at the truck stop clothes she'd discarded on the tiled floor of the bathroom. The sweatpants should be okay to wear again, but she'd bled through the shirt. It didn't matter in the big scheme of things. Because Vadim was right. She wasn't sure how long she'd slept in the shower, but she felt less fuzzy now. Enough so that she knew talking to the police in Vegas and at least documenting her injury was the smart thing. She couldn't believe how out of it, how purely panicked she'd been. "Okay. If you know where Vadim's First Aid kit is, I'll grab it."

He just snorted and pointed to the marble-topped counter. "Sit there. I'll be back."

Normally a forceful or demanding tone from a stranger would get a rise out of her, but it was a relief to let someone else take over. At least temporarily. Adrenaline might be jagging through her, but she was still weak and shaky. As he left the room, she grabbed the sweatpants off the floor and tugged them on. Then she held the towel up to her chest as she sat on the counter.

Turning sideways, she looked at her exposed body in the mirror. The wound was still red and trickles of blood were still streaming down her side. Damn it, she'd probably get the blood on her pants now. She slid off the countertop as Roman walked back in with a small red and white kit in one of his big hands.

"You doing okay?" he asked, his voice strong and soothing, taking away some of her edginess.

She clutched the towel to her chest, not caring that her back was exposed. "Yeah. I just realized I shouldn't have put my sweatpants on so soon. Not until after I patch up."

He nodded and turned around. "Strip 'em and tell me when you're ready."

She blinked at that tone that brooked no argument. "You can just leave the kit with me."

"It makes more sense for me to bandage you. The wound is in an uncomfortable place." He shrugged. "But you can do what you want."

She liked that he wasn't pushing her, his actions making her trust him more than words ever could. "You're right. Hold on." She shimmied the pants off before hopping back up on the counter. Her back and part of her butt were visible in the mirror as she held the towel over her front and around her non-wounded side, but she didn't have enough energy to care about partial nudity at this point.

When he turned around, he paused for a second, his gaze sweeping over her in a very non-clinical fashion. He did it so quickly she wondered if he was even aware of it. A moment later, he was at her side. If Vadim vouched for him, she was going to trust him. There was something intrinsically solid about him too. She couldn't put her finger on it, but there it was, the most primal part of her brain telling her she'd be safe with this man. Not that he in any way or shape seemed safe. No, he had a dangerous edge to him, but he wouldn't hurt her.

"Hold your arm up while I clean your wound, okay?" he asked in a surprisingly gentle voice.

She did as he said, watching as he opened the kit.

"So Neal Lynch is the name of the man who shot you?" he asked as he began pulling out antiseptic and bandages.

"Vadim told you his last name?" She looked away from him, facing forward as she spoke.

"Yeah. This might sting for a second, but I'm going to clean the wound."

"It won't hurt more than getting shot," she muttered.

Roman laughed, the bold sound taking her off guard, rolling through her like a warm, soothing balm. "You're right about that. And you're damn lucky that Lynch fucker wasn't a better shot. I don't even think you'll need stitches."

"Have you ever had stitches?" she asked, mainly just to make conversation and steer away from talking about Neal. Even thinking about that monster, the way he'd gunned down Hugh, made her throat tighten and tears well up again. She didn't want to have another breakdown. Not yet. Not until Neal was behind bars.

Roman let out a short chuckle as he put something cool on her wound. "Yeah. Too many times to count."

"From your time in the Marines?" She bit back a hiss as he laid the bandage over her wound. The contact made all the muscles in her body tighten.

"I got a few there too, but mostly from growing up with a brother in the South. We spent a lot of time outdoors and bruises, cuts, and broken bones just seemed to happen." He paused and looked up at her as his long fingers still held the bandage in place.

Turning, she looked at him. "What?"

"There's no tape in the kit, just a wrap to secure the bandage." He held up a small roll of gauzy, cling roll. "I'm going to need to wrap this around you to keep the bandage in place."

"Okay . . . oh." It took her a moment to realize what he was saying. He'd already seen her naked and it was probably the blood loss, but she was beyond caring if he saw her naked again. Okay, she didn't care *too* much. "Turn away for a second."

When he turned his head, she dropped the towel onto her lap so she was partially covered and crossed her arm over her breasts.

Moving quickly, he secured the bandage around her middle, his callused fingers grazing over her skin with efficiency. She found herself oddly disappointed that his hands didn't linger. Which yeah, told her all she needed to know about her mindset right now. She needed sleep and a hospital. And probably some food considering she'd barely eaten in days. When he was done, he turned away again so she could pull her pants back on. As she straightened, she swayed a little, but recovered quickly, clutching onto the counter with her free hand as she held the towel to her chest.

But Roman didn't miss a thing. His eyebrows drew together as he slid an arm around her waist and under her legs. She nearly let out a yelp as he lifted her off the ground. She lifted the towel up to partially cover herself.

"What are you doing?" A thread of panic slid through her veins. Vadim trusted this man and Roman had shown himself to be nothing but kind, if a little bossy, since finding her in his friend's home. But she couldn't fight off her internal distress.

"You look as if you're about to pass out on your feet," he said, striding from the bathroom. "So I'm getting you food and one of Angel's shirts before we head to the hospital. Unless you want to wear your bloody one?" He glanced down at her as he made his way out into the bedroom, the look in his eyes unreadable.

Taylor shook her head and curled into him, hooking her arm around his neck and burrowing a little closer. He sucked in a breath, the action barely noticeable but being impossibly close she didn't miss it.

His jaw clenched tight as he set her at one of the high-backed chairs at the island in the kitchen. Without looking at her, he turned and strode from the room, the bulge of his weapon visible at his back. Even though she couldn't see it, she knew it was a gun. It didn't matter that he was clearly trained, the sight made her shiver. She wrapped her arms over her breasts as she waited, but luckily he didn't take long.

Less than a minute later he returned with a long-sleeved, black T-shirt with a small Nike symbol on it. It looked like a workout shirt. "You're a little smaller than Angel but this should fit. I just grabbed the first thing I could find." He seemed a little uncomfortable as he set it on the counter next to her.

She started to thank him, but then his entire body pulled taut, a frown pulling at his already harsh-looking mouth. "Put the shirt on," he ordered as he withdrew his gun.

Fear spiked through her. He seemed on alert for some reason. She watched as he strode toward the door that led to the utility room with the grace of a jungle predator. She'd never seen anyone so big move with such incredible fluidity. Without pause she tugged the T-shirt on, wincing as she had to lift her hands up to pull it over her head. She might be smaller than Angel, but her breasts were clearly bigger. The shirt pulled across her chest, making it clear that she didn't have a bra on, but no way was she putting hers back on. Part of it had dried blood on it and she wasn't sure if it would rub against the bandage.

Worried about why Roman had gone out to the garage, she headed for the utility room. Two loud pops from somewhere made her jump.

Gunfire.

Fear for Roman's safety punched through her as she raced out the door.

CHAPTER FIVE

Roman slowly exited the utility room into the garage, the low hum of an engine from outside clear. At first he hadn't been sure he'd heard anything, but now it was unmistakable.

Weapon drawn, he hurried to the partially-open garage door. The Pinto blocked his legs so he used it for cover as he laid on the ground and peered out. Behind the beater car and to the right of his truck he saw wheels.

He slipped out under the left side of the garage and used the Pinto as cover as he crept along the side of it. Still crouching low, he looked through the windows and saw an SUV. Though the windows were tinted, the sun was setting behind it so he could see inside well enough. One man was outlined in the driver's seat, but no one else was visible.

The driver's door opened and a man got out. A ball cap was pulled low over his forehead but stray sandy-blond hair peeked out under the sides. From what Roman could see he had on a long-sleeved, brown shirt. Sunglasses covered his eyes, hiding a good portion of his face, as he looked around, scanning the property. He stepped out from around the protection of the SUV, rounding the front of it.

Keeping his weapon lowered, Roman stood, using the Pinto as a barrier. "Who are you?"

The man tensed, but didn't make any sudden moves as he zeroed in on Roman. "I'm looking for Vadim. You him?"

Vadim didn't give many people his address. Hell, Roman was pretty sure he even had packages delivered to his office at The Serafina. So a stranger shouldn't have it. "How'd you get this address?"

The man took a slight step back toward the driver's door. It was subtle, but Roman noted it.

"Get off this property before I call the police," he continued when the man didn't move.

The man's body language changed, the nuances small but Roman watched as he stilled, his body taut. He didn't like pinning his weapon on anyone, but his gut told him it was necessary. He lifted his arm, aiming it at the guy's center mass. "I won't tell you again. Get the fuck out of here. Now."

The man paused once before hurrying to the driver's door. Roman kept his weapon trained on him the entire time. The engine was still running so the driver got in and reversed. As he did, he turned the vehicle back so that the driver's side faced Roman. The sunlight glinted off the windshield, making him flinch.

He took a step to the side, back toward the garage to avoid being blinded, when he saw that the driver's side window was down. He couldn't see a weapon and wasn't going to open fire on someone without just cause. But instinct had him taking cover behind the car.

Pop. Pop.

Two thunking sounds on the garage door spurred him into action. Rolling under the door, he shifted so that the position of the Pinto gave him cover. Standing, he slammed the garage door down. The sound of screeching tires told him the guy was leaving. But for how long? And did he have backup? Roman wasn't sticking around like a sitting duck waiting to find out. He'd call the cops but only as soon as he got Taylor away from here and to the hospital. Racing toward the utility room, he hurried inside.

Taylor started to swing a broom handle at him, but froze with the end of it in midair, her arm dropping to her side. Her blue eyes were wide as she scanned him, likely for wounds. "Are you okay? What happened?"

He hooked his hand under her elbow and steered her into the kitchen. "Man who said he was looking for Vadim shot at me before racing off. Sandy-blond hair, medium build, maybe five-eleven. Driving a black SUV. Ring any bells?"

She bit her bottom lip as she moved with him, clutching the broom tightly in her hand. "Maybe. Gordon Simpson is the man I saw at the police station. He's got blond hair, but it's pretty light. And I don't know how tall he is. Taller than me."

He snorted. "Most people are probably taller than you."

To his surprise, she laughed, the musical quality of it taking him off guard. "True."

"Grab all your blood-stained clothes and anything you need to take with you. We're not coming back here," he informed her, gently pushing her toward the bedroom as he made his way to the foyer.

Vadim's house was all glass, wood and high ceilings with exposed beams. Roman knew he had a special film over his windows that made it difficult to see inside. The foyer was one of the best vantage points because of the long, slim windows on the sides of the front door. So Roman surveyed the front yard, driveway, and all he saw was dust kicking up in the distance where the SUV had fled.

There was a risk leaving with Taylor, but it was calculated. Because if they stayed, they had a higher chance of being attacked. Roman knew there was a definite potential for an ambush as they left the property but he didn't think it would happen. A single man had shown up, obviously not expecting Roman to be here and ready for him. No, the guy would be leaving and regrouping and possibly getting more backup. Roman didn't want to stay here and find out. There were just too many unknowns at this point. He turned away front the window at the sound of Taylor approaching.

"I've got it all." She lifted two plastic bags of her things.

He nodded. Normally he'd take a woman's bags for her, but he wasn't putting his weapon down. "We're going to leave with you driving my truck and I'm going to follow you in the Pinto. Once we reach the end of Vadim's driveway,"—which was a mile long—"we're going to head east. There's a gas station about three-quarters of a mile down the road. We're going to leave the Pinto there and take my truck to the hospital." His truck had bullet-resistant windows so he knew she'd be safe inside.

And he was armed and had taken multiple defensive driving courses so he wasn't worried about himself.

"Okay, but why are we leaving the Pinto?"

"Did you steal it?" She hadn't said how she'd gotten here when she'd spoken to Vadim, but the woman had broken into the man's house with impressive ease. Somehow he didn't think stealing a car would be an issue for her. And a Pinto didn't seem like her style.

Her cheeks flushed, the natural caramel of her skin tone darkening to a crimson. "How'd you know?"

"Lucky guess," he muttered, pulling his keys out of his pocket and handing them to her. "You okay to drive?"

She nodded as she clasped them in her palm. "Roman, I don't know how I can ever thank you." Tears filled her eyes, but she blinked them away. "You don't even know me and I just . . . thank you."

Any kind of praise made him as uncomfortable as crying women did, so he just nodded. "No problem," he grunted and turned on his heel. He was going to reset Vadim's alarm, then they were getting the hell out of here. And he was going to keep Taylor safe no matter what. He couldn't explain what it was, but he felt the strangest pull toward her, his attraction for her sharpening each second that passed.

* * *

Taylor didn't understand why she had to wear the stupid, itchy hospital gown when she knew she wouldn't be staying. But the scary nurse had insisted and Roman had been no help whatsoever. Shifting against the bed, she crossed her arms over her chest and frowned.

"The gowns aren't that bad," Roman murmured, his eyes lit with amusement from his perch near the window.

Still no smile though. She wondered if he actually knew how. His arms were crossed over his massive chest, those different-colored eyes pinned on her. It was dark outside but the room lights glinted off his hair, highlighting the natural auburn throughout his darker brown hair. He was . . . ridiculously handsome. So much so that it left her feeling unbalanced. And he hadn't left her side.

"You want to wear it then?"

His lips pulled together. "I'm not the one who got shot."

Almost against her will she found her gaze drawn to his mouth. Damn it, what was wrong with her? Now that she was coming down from that insane adrenaline high, she should be ready to pass out again. Instead she found herself captivated by Roman . . . "Hey, what's your last name?" she blurted, realizing she had no idea. And she really wanted to know.

She could barely remember the last guy she'd slept with, let alone been this attracted to. Okay, she didn't think she'd ever been attracted to anyone as much as Roman. The timing was awful, making her feel even crappier. Her friend was dead and she was having annoying feelings for a stranger.

"MacNeil." Now his gaze dropped to her mouth and his eyes heated with a surprising intensity.

So much so that she squirmed against the starchy sheets of the hospital bed. She opened her mouth, ready to say something—anything—when the door opened.

A huge, dark-haired man wearing black slacks, a light blue dress shirt with no tie and a police badge hooked to his belt stepped in. The man could have been a football player he was so big. He nodded once at Roman, who straightened and made a beeline for her bed.

The action surprised her, but Roman moved in like he was her personal bodyguard as he smoothly slid in place directly next to her head. She looked up at him and smiled gratefully. One corner of his mouth quirked up and she felt it all the way to her toes.

God, she was a hot mess. She shouldn't be noticing anyone in a sexual way right now. Turning back to the man she guessed was here to see her, she forced a smile. "I assume you're Detective Hurley?"

He nodded and grabbed a seat on the opposite side of her bed. "Yes, ma'am. Detective Cody Hurley but you can call me either. I answer to both." He gave her a charming grin she was sure usually got the ladies ruffled. He probably used it when interrogating female suspects.

"Okay, Cody. You can call me Taylor."

Cody pulled out a small, spiral notepad and a pen. She let out a nervous laugh, which sounded almost maniacal even to herself. Jeez, she needed to get a grip. When Roman placed a gentle hand on her shoulder, she reached up and briefly put her hand over his without thinking. She rarely depended on anyone for anything and she wasn't sure why she was leaning on him now other than it was simply instinctual. Which, yeah, she knew was crazy. But she didn't care because if Vadim trusted him then that was good enough for her, and the man's presence was comforting.

The detective raised his eyebrows. "Is something funny?"

"No. I sometimes have weird social responses when I get nervous. I didn't think detectives actually used notepads. It seems like something off of television and it's why I laughed." Even though it wasn't funny at all. *Stop talking*, she ordered herself. At least she wasn't laughing like a crazy person anymore so that was good.

He gave a real smile. "Well, we do. So do patrolmen. It's how we keep track of everything. So, I already talked to the nurse and she assures me you've been shot. We're going to send your medical records over to Oceanside for documentation."

A sharp sense of relief invaded Taylor as he continued.

"I've already talked to a friend on the force with Oceanside PD about your presence here. After what Roman told me about the shooter at Vadim's place and about you being in shock and fleeing to Vegas, they know you're not on the run."

"What about Vadim's house?" Roman asked quietly, giving her a comforting squeeze. She was glad he'd left his hand there. It made her feel grounded.

"Got a team there now digging the bullets out of the garage door. Just like you said." Cody's expression was grim. "I'll talk to you about it in a sec."

There was slight movement next to her and she guessed Roman nodded because Cody turned all his attention back to her. "I'm going to be honest with you. Running makes you look bad, but with these extenuating circumstances, it's understandable. Roman gave me a rundown of what's going on, but I want you to go over everything for me. Start to finish. You're going to have to repeat all of this to the guys in Oceanside, but I'm going to relay everything to them too. The more details they have before you get back, the better."

She took a deep breath and told Cody everything from the reason she'd shown up early at work all the way until Roman had found her passed out with a bottle of vodka. The only thing she'd left out was that she'd stolen a Pinto. She just said she'd fled. That was all he needed to know right now. And she also didn't say that she'd broken into Vadim's place, just that she had the code, which actually wasn't a lie. She'd *guessed* the code. The little thing with the garage door wasn't important."

When she was done, Cody was silent for a long moment as he wrote in his notepad. Finally he said, "Gordon Simpson is the name of the man you saw waiting outside the police department?"

"Yes. And I don't know that he's involved with Neal, but he was there at the police station and I was terrified. I'd just been shot. Maybe I panicked for no reason but it was too weird seeing him there. As part of the security team for Powers Group he's done work with Neal before, but he's also done work with Hugh too." She supposed there could have been a reason for his presence at the police station but she hadn't been in the frame of mind to find out what it was. Not when she'd been fearful for her life.

Cody just nodded and made another note. He started to say something when his phone buzzed on his belt. He pulled it out and looked at it. With a frown, he said, "I've gotta take this."

When the door shut behind him, Roman dropped his hand from her shoulder and moved around so that he was facing her. He sat on the edge of the bed, his expression unreadable. It was a little unnerving. "If Cody doesn't ask you how you got here, don't mention the Pinto. Later, if you have to, be honest, but right now keep it quiet."

"I will." Because she definitely agreed with him.

The detective stepped back in the room, his phone still in his hand. "I'm going to relay everything you told me to Oceanside and I'll need you both to come down to the station tomorrow to give official statements about the shooting today." His head tilted to the side a fraction as he glanced at Roman. "Can I talk to you outside?"

Alarm bells went off in her head, but Taylor reminded herself that not all cops were bad, that this man was going out of his way to help her because Vadim and Roman had asked.

Roman nodded and stood. "Yeah."

Cody focused on her once again. "It goes without saying, but don't leave town yet."

She sighed. "I won't."

"Where are you staying?"

"With me," Roman said as he came to stand next to the detective.

Well that was news to her and she certainly wasn't going to argue. So she nodded. "With Roman."

That seemed to be good enough for the detective because he just grunted and held open the door for Roman.

Less than five minutes later Roman returned alone. Okay that was good. It probably meant the detective wasn't coming back to arrest her. She knew the truth was on her side, but fear was a living thing inside her. "Everything okay?" Her voice was high-pitched and uneven so she cleared her throat.

"Yeah. He just wanted to go over the description of the shooter and other details. They're going to see if they can catch him on CCTVs close to the area. Though I doubt that's going to happen since I didn't get his license plate. Vadim lives too far out from the city."

The fear inside her spiked even more. "Maybe I shouldn't stay with you." Not when she clearly had a target on her back. "I don't want to put you in danger." Vadim had said the man had been a Marine, so he was trained, but it still worried her.

He snorted and headed for the door again. "I'm going to see if I can find a doctor and get you released."

After she'd been officially admitted, examined and prescribed antibiotics, the doctor had already told her he wouldn't need to keep her for further observation. She could stay overnight if she thought she needed it, but she'd much rather stay at Roman's. Roman had already told her that the truck he'd been driving was a company vehicle and the address listed on the title was for the hotel and casino he worked at; The Serafina. So if the shooter tried to track him down using the truck's license plate, that guy would be out of luck. It was actually the only reason she would stay with Roman because if there was a chance she could put him in danger, she simply wouldn't do it. Even if he was deadly and trained.

It still stunned her how kind he was being. Yeah, she knew it was because of his relationship with Vadim but still, it was amazing. She was a stranger and he'd stepped up to the plate to protect her, even letting her stay at his place. That told her all she needed to know about the type of man Roman MacNeil was.

A very rare one—the kind of man she wouldn't mind getting to know better.

CHAPTER SIX

Taylor opened her eyes with a start and nearly jerked upright in the soft bed. The shadows and furniture in the room were wrong and it took her a second to remember where she was. Roman's house. In his brother's bed since Logan was still out of town for his job. They had two guest rooms but one was an office and the other had an uncomfortable looking futon—to discourage guests, Roman had said. So he'd given her his brother's bed.

Until he'd told her, she hadn't known that both Roman and his brother Logan worked private security for billionaire Wyatt Christiansen. It certainly explained the extremely large house they lived in. She knew a little about the Vegas real estate market so it wasn't hard to imagine they'd gotten it for a steal, but even so, the neighborhood was beautiful.

Her racing heart calmed a fraction as her eyes adjusted to the dimness. Faint light filtered through a set of wooden blinds on the window behind the king-sized bed. According to the clock on the nightstand it was six in the morning. By the time they'd arrived at Roman's place last night it had been late and she'd passed out almost immediately. Now, she couldn't seem to turn her mind off. Sitting up, she was relieved that her wound didn't hurt as much.

After brushing her teeth with the extra toothbrush Roman had given her, washing her face and inspecting her wound, she headed for his room. It was early and she felt bad that she'd likely wake him up, but she needed a favor. Fast.

His room was two doors down from Logan's. She knocked softly on the door and was surprised when it opened seconds later. Roman's hair looked more brown than auburn in the dimness. Even though it was on the short side, it was ruffled, but he looked wide awake, his eyes piercing in their intensity. From his alertness she didn't think she'd woken him up. "You okay?" he asked softly.

For a moment her gaze dipped to his bare chest and abs. The man was pure muscle, all lean lines and angles with a few scars interspersed on his skin for good measure. She guessed he must have gotten them when he'd been in the Marines. Maybe during combat or training. He was like a walking billboard of what hotness looked like. She had the insane urge to reach out and trace over the dips and striations. Forcing her gaze to his, she said, "Yes. I hate to bug you but can I use your laptop? I thought of something as soon as I woke up." More like the thought had woken her up. And she couldn't let the sight of Roman's ridiculous body distract her no matter how delicious the man was.

He stepped back so she could enter. "Give me a sec." He flipped on the lamp on his nightstand, illuminating his room. He had a king-sized bed like his brother but his was platform style. Very minimalist. So was the rest of his room with sleek, dark wood furniture, including a bookshelf overflowing with non-fiction books. He headed for the bookshelf and pulled a thin laptop from the top of it. "Is this about what happened to your boss?" he asked as he flipped it open and sat on the edge of his bed.

She hesitated for a moment, but he was letting her use his computer and was basically keeping her safe at his home. He deserved an answer. "Yes. Maybe I should wait for the police to sort things out, but I know Neal stole a ton of money from the company and I don't want to let him get away with it. Now that I know it's him and not Hugh—that bastard tried to make it look like his own partner had taken it—I think I can track down the funds. I just need to look at a few of his personal accounts."

Roman frowned as he looked up at her but he patted the edge of the bed for her to sit beside him. "Wouldn't Neal have already locked you out of the system?"

She snorted and sat next to Roman, subtly inhaling that masculine, woodsy scent that seemed stronger in his room. As if the air and sheets were permeated with it. "I'm sure he did but I've got multiple backdoors into the entire system. I work closely with the IT department but even they don't know about this."

Roman's eyebrows raised but he handed her the laptop. "What exactly do you do for Powers Group?"

"I don't really have one set thing that I do," she said, pulling up a browser and typing in the website she needed. She felt so level-headed this morning and couldn't believe she hadn't thought of this yesterday. Well, she could believe it considering she'd seen her friend die and she'd been shot—and she'd gone on the run. "This won't come back on you, by the way. No one will be able to trace what I've done. Not that it'll matter because I'm taking the money Neal stole once I track it down and diverting it to a secure company account. It'll just sit there until the police figure out everything." Her fingers flew across the keyboard as she talked. "As far as what I do, I have a Masters in Computer Science and I do a lot of design for the company, but . . . I really do a lot of investigations for Hugh. Or, I did."

She swallowed hard, shaking away the dark path her mind wanted to take. She refused to get sucked into depression. Not when she had a chance to take back what that bastard Neal had stolen and clear Hugh's name. Because she didn't think Neal was above trying to say Hugh had stolen from the company and attacked him or some crap. It would be a stupid defense considering he'd shot her, but she wasn't going to let him even try to drag Hugh's name through the mud.

"Anyway, I look into any company that Powers Group might do business with, including owners' personal finances or personal anything. For the most part Hugh was all business, pretty cutthroat when he needed to be, but he also had a huge heart. When I found out this construction mogul had a bunch of arrests for domestic violence, Hugh refused to do business with him."

"Damn." Roman sounded impressed.

"I know, right. Hugh was . . . he was just a good guy." Her throat tightened again and she stopped talking, unable to go on.

"You loved him." His voice was quiet, speculative.

Taylor paused and glanced at Roman to find him watching her intently. "Well, yeah. Not romantically or anything but he was like a dad to me. He never had kids and he took me under his wing right out of college." Taylor was pretty certain Hugh had viewed her as a daughter. Or maybe that was just wishful thinking, but she knew he'd loved her too. And it broke her heart to be thinking of him in the past tense. Well, she was going to get justice for him no matter what.

Looking away from Roman before she started crying, she focused on her task, infiltrating Neal's multiple email accounts and files he thought he'd hidden. She nearly snorted at his stupidity and saved them all to a secret company Cloud account only she and Hugh had access to. Well, just her now.

After finding those files it was just a matter of time before tracing the trail of diverted money. She wasn't able to guess his password, but she was able to reset it using one of his email accounts. The bank sent a 'reset password' email to him and she reset it all right. She laughed to herself as she did it, feeling insanely pleased that she was able to do this much to Neal. A man like him only cared about money and she was taking all of this away from him. Sure, he had personal accounts but he was stealing for a reason. He needed the cash because of his gambling debts. She wasn't sure who he owed money to and she didn't particularly care. She just cared that he wasn't going to hurt the company or take anything else that didn't belong to him. As soon as she'd transferred all the money, she changed the passwords in all his accounts to different ones, effectively locking him out of everything. She wanted him to know exactly what she'd done. Even if he called his bank and got back into his account online, all his money was still gone.

Next she locked *him* out of the Powers Group system.

"And fuck you," she muttered as she finished the last keystrokes. When she was done, she closed everything down and gently shut the laptop. She looked up to find Roman watching her with a mixture of humor and something else. It was almost like he was impressed. "What?" she asked self-consciously, tucking a lock of hair behind her ear.

"You just did a pretty impressive evil genius laugh." His lips twitched again, the humor in his beautiful eyes clear.

For a long moment she watched him, completely drawn into his gaze. She felt her cheeks heating up. "I did *not* do an evil genius laugh."

A dark eyebrow lifted. "You kinda did. And it was hot."

Her eyes widened at the same time his did. As if he was surprised he'd said it. A spiral of heat swirled through her as she watched him. "You think it was hot?"

He cleared his throat and even though she was just getting to know him, his response told her he might not be big on flirting. Which was fine with her because she sucked at it. She didn't do coy well. Hell, she sometimes struggled with normal social conversations. Computers were easier to deal with than people and their mixed signals. Feeling awkward when he didn't say anything else, she slid the laptop onto the bed behind her. "Well, thanks for letting me use your computer."

Taking her completely by surprise—and that was an understatement—he leaned in close, covering the distance between them, obviously giving her time to pull back. He watched her carefully, his eyes intense as he brushed his lips over hers. As if he was testing the waters.

It was like an electric current jolted through her at the contact. He felt it too. She saw it in his eyes. Refusing to pass up this opportunity, she pressed her lips fully to his, making her intent clear. She didn't want a weak, barely-there kiss.

Not when this brief contact already had her nipples tightening and heat rushing between her legs. If this was happening, she was getting the real thing. He took over, one of his big hands sliding up to cup the back of her head as his mouth devoured hers. The grip on her head was tight, dominating and had her moaning into his mouth as a shudder rolled through her. He was so different from other men she'd kissed or dated. Not that they were remotely dating, but even her response to him was different. She felt as if he was heating her up from the inside out.

His tongue pressed insistently against the seam of her lips, demanding entrance as his other hand slid up to cradle her cheek. She loved the way he held her in place, as if he thought she might flee.

No way was that happening.

Unable to stop herself, even if she'd wanted to—and she most definitely didn't—she slid her hands up his bare chest, another shudder rippling through her as her fingers skimmed all those rock-hard surfaces. It was like the man had been created from marble.

As their tongues danced together, Roman withdrew his hands from her head and face. Before she realized what he was doing, he fisted her hips and she found herself straddling his lap. His erection rubbed against her covered mound, the friction still amazing even through the too-big sweatpants he'd let her borrow and his plaid boxer shorts.

He kept his hands on the outside of her clothes, but slid one carefully over her non-injured side, and the other over her hip and down her leg, as if he was memorizing the way she felt.

She lifted up slightly on her knees, rubbing herself over his hard length, loving the sensation of it where she was wet and needy. He groaned into her mouth, his big body shuddering underneath her.

It was as if her entire body was lit up with need and hunger. Sure it had been a while since she'd been with anyone, but she couldn't ever remember being this turned on by a kiss. Maybe it was the emotional rollercoaster she'd been on the last couple days but she really didn't think so.

It was because of Roman.

She clutched his shoulders and started to push him back against the bed, but he took over completely, rolling them so that she was under him. Something hard rubbed against her back and it took her a moment to realize it was the laptop.

Making an annoyed growling sound, he grabbed it and shoved it somewhere above their heads on the bed. Rolling her hips into him, she loved the sensation of his erection stroking over her. His weight was heavy and perfect, his masculine scent addictive.

When a low ringing sound penetrated her brain, she wondered what was going on when Roman pulled back from her, breathing hard. He stared down at her as the ringing continued. What was that? His alarm? She blinked, feeling dazed as he cursed and slid off her body. Immediately she mourned the loss of his big body covering hers.

"Better be fucking life and death," he muttered as he moved to his nightstand.

She sat back up and turned around to see him picking up his cell phone. She'd been so focused on Roman she'd barely been aware of anything else.

"Hey, Hurley," he said, his voice tight, turning to face her.

Taylor slid off the bed and straightened, wrapping her arms around herself. If the detective was calling this early she didn't know if that was good or bad. Only able to listen to half of the conversation, she didn't garner much since Roman responded a lot with one word answers or grunts.

As soon as he hung up, she practically pounced on him. "Well?"

"They dug a bullet out of the back of the elevator. Hurley said the lead detective is pissed the crime scene guys missed it the first go around, but I guess the elevator has a weird texture?"

She nodded. "Yeah, it's all chrome and nickel with weird rises in the texture. It's always made me think of medieval armor. Did they find anything else?"

"Blood on the bullet. They're testing it now and putting a rush on it. Since it goes against Neal's story, combined with the traces of blood splatter they found with luminol, you're going to be cleared soon. Hurley wants us to come down to the station to make a statement about what happened yesterday, then the Oceanside PD wants you to come in. They're going to give you time to return to the city voluntarily and they're bringing Neal in for more questioning. They can hold him long enough to do the blood test. As long as the evidence corroborates with your story—and I know it will—you'll be cleared of everything."

She perched on the edge of the bed as she digested his words. She was innocent so she wasn't worried about being cleared, but there would be so much to do now, including planning Hugh's funeral. That thought brought up a fresh wave of sadness so she stood. "Do you think I have time for coffee before we head to the station?" Part of her wanted to finish what she and Roman had just started, but the realistic part of her brain knew it was probably for the best they didn't do anything else.

Roman nodded and glanced at the clock. "Yeah. My brother should be home soon too. I texted him and asked him to bring you some clothes so I apologize in advance if they're . . . not your style."

She lifted her eyebrows at that, but didn't question him. "Thank you. Again. I know you're doing all this for Vadim, but still—"

"Stop thanking me. This stopped being about Vadim a while ago." His voice was raspy and an octave lower than normal as he watched her.

Oh. Okay, maybe she really did want to finish what they'd just started. "Um..." She didn't know what to say, but thankfully he saved her.

"I'm going to grab a quick shower," he said, shifting as if he was uncomfortable. It took about a second for her to realize why and her face flamed once again. "The coffee maker is the one-cup kind and easy to use."

"I saw it last night and it's the same kind I have." She seriously needed a dose of caffeine. Once she left his room, she let out a big breath she hadn't realized she'd been holding. The man lit her nerves on fire and had the ability to distract her even from the worst situation. She wasn't sure how she felt about that. For all she knew what she was feeling was because of everything that had happened, but something told her she'd be feeling this way about Roman no matter what. The timing sucked too because she had way too much to deal with right now without worrying about her reaction to him. She'd be leaving town in a couple hours anyway.

* * *

Roman strode down the stairs, pausing when he heard his brother's voice and Taylor's following laughter. He was surprised his brother was home so soon. The shower he'd taken had done nothing to douse the hunger raging through him. He hadn't expected her to knock on his door so early this morning.

Hadn't expected to kiss her.

And he hadn't expected the primal reaction he was still coming to grips with. He'd wanted to take her right on his bed, a place he never brought women. His few and far between fucks were always at the woman's place or in a hotel when he was out of town. That was one thing he and his twin had in common, they never brought women back to their place.

But he'd liked the thought of Taylor in his bed, underneath him, moaning out his name as he brought her pleasure. Way too much. Fuck. He scrubbed a hand over his face as he reached the bottom of the stairs.

When he entered the kitchen he found Taylor leaning against one of the granite countertops, a coffee cup in hand. She was dressed in clothes his brother had presumably brought for her. Tight jeans that were a little too long and a plain black V-neck T-shirt that stretched across her breasts. He found his gaze lingering on those full breasts and once again, his dick decided to wake up. Damn it, he'd just jerked off in the shower to thoughts of Taylor—something he should probably feel bad about, but didn't—he should be fine, but one look at her and he was getting hard again.

Roman focused on his brother because it was better than staring at Taylor like some horny teenager.

"Where's Charlie?" Logan asked.

"Oh, had Brannon pick her up after we got back from the hospital." Nicholas Brannon worked security at the Serafina. Since Roman wasn't sure what was going to happen with Taylor and he'd known his brother would be exhausted after his last job, he'd wanted to make sure the dog was taken care of for a while. And Brannon would spoil the dog more than Vadim. Clearing his throat, he continued. "Thanks for the clothes. Did you get her a sweater?" It was chilly outside.

Logan gave him a strange look and nodded at one of the chairs at the island where a black cardigan was slung across the back. "Yeah. Taylor tells me you two are headed to the police station."

"Yeah." He'd been scarce on information about her, only telling his twin the basics when he'd asked him to bring her clothes. And that wasn't like him. But he felt a strange proprietary sense toward her. Even where his twin was concerned.

"Should I come along?" There was a note in his twin's voice he recognized. It was subtle, but it almost sounded like Logan was baiting him. Or at least trying to push him for some reason. Probably because he'd been so secretive about Taylor and the whole situation.

"Nah, you just got off a long stretch. We'll be fine." It was true that Logan had just come off a longer than normal security job for their boss, Wyatt. He'd been on an out of town trip and taken on more responsibility since Wyatt's normal right-hand man, Jay Wentworth, had some old SEAL buddies in town for the week and had taken off. Roman didn't really care that Logan had come off a job though, he wanted Taylor all to himself, not around his charming twin.

His brother's dark eyes narrowed a fraction, but he nodded. "All right."

Roman looked back at Taylor and his heart rate kicked up about a hundred notches. "We've got insulated cups if you want to bring your coffee with you."

She shook her head, her cheeks slightly flushed. "I'm good, but thanks. I just need to grab my shoes from upstairs and I'll be ready to go."

He nodded, watching as she said something else to his brother, then headed out of the kitchen. Even though it was instinct to trail after her with his gaze, he didn't. Instead, he headed for the coffee pot and grabbed a mug from the cabinet above it.

"What's going on with you? Why don't you want me going along?" Logan asked.

Roman shrugged, but his shoulders were stiff. "I know you've got better things to do."

"This isn't about Taylor?" His brother's voice was dry.

"No. I'm ready to get rid of her." A big fucking lie. One that tasted bitter in his mouth.

Logan snorted. "Bullshit."

He glanced over his shoulder at his brother. "You think I like dealing with this situation?"

"I think you like her and you don't want me around."

Damn his brother and their fucking twin bond. He could never hide anything from Logan. All he had to do was walk into a room and his twin just got a vibe for how he was feeling. It was the same for Roman. They'd driven their mother insane when they'd been kids.

"I also think salt is going to taste nasty in your coffee." Logan tilted his chin toward the open cabinet where Roman had his fingers clenched around a container of salt.

Damn, he was distracted. He let it go and grabbed the sugar before turning to face his brother. "You've got a smug look on your face."

Logan lifted his hands and framed his face with his fingers into a square. "This handsome mug?"

The corners of Roman's mouth lifted. "Yeah. Why?"

"Why? Because you like this girl enough that you brought her back to our place."

"I only brought her here to keep her safe. And she slept in *your* bed." After that kiss they'd just shared, he really wished it had been in his bed instead.

"Too bad I wasn't there. She wouldn't have gotten any sleep."

Before he realized he'd moved, Roman took a step forward—and stopped when Logan's face split into a wide grin.

"You're a dick," Roman muttered.

Logan's grin just grew wider. "Roman and Taylor, sitting in a tree—"

He groaned. "You're so fucking infantile. Seriously, I don't know how you ever get laid."

Logan shrugged and moved past him, grabbing Roman's mug, like he normally did. Roman started making another cup as his brother said, "You know how. It's this handsome face and charming personality."

"You're in a mood this morning. Good trip?" he asked as the machine started brewing another cup.

"Trip was fine. I'm just glad you met someone normal."

"You spent maybe ten minutes with her."

"Yeah and I can already tell she's a hundred times sweeter and saner than that bitch—"

"Logan." Roman didn't want to talk about his ex. Didn't want to think about her. Not because he was still hung up on her, he just didn't want to compare Taylor to Justina.

It felt wrong on too many levels. Mainly because it reminded him what an idiot he'd been. And the two women were in completely different leagues. Taylor was . . . fucking amazing. She was beautiful, yeah, but she'd held up well under some shitty circumstances. Not only that, but she was a fighter. Her determination to bring down the man who'd killed her friend was impressive. Not once had she complained about her circumstances.

His brother shrugged again. "All I'm saying is, I like Taylor."

"Yeah, me too." Probably too much. Now he needed to get his game face on and get her to the police station. So far it seemed as if the evidence was backing up her story—and he believed her anyway, her grief over Hugh was too damn real—but there was still a threat out there. Whoever had shot at him yesterday had likely been there for her.

Just because the Oceanside PD was going to bring Neal Lynch in didn't mean that whoever had come after Taylor would stop gunning for her. If that bastard Neal had sent someone after her, they might not stop until she was silenced.

That was happening over his dead body.

CHAPTER SEVEN

Neal groaned as the sound of a phone ringing cut through the quiet room. He recognized the ringtone, otherwise he'd have ignored it. Opening his eyes, he looked over at the naked woman in his bed. Sunlight from a couple open blinds streamed through, highlighting her face. Her body was perfectly toned but she had more wrinkles around her mouth and eyes than he remembered last night when he'd picked her up. But he'd needed some quick stress relief and she'd been cheaper than buying a professional for the evening. All he'd had to do was buy her a few drinks.

Ignoring her presence, he grabbed his cell phone from the nightstand and answered it. She didn't even stir as he left the room. "Yeah?" His voice was hoarse and raspy. Probably shouldn't have drank so much last night. Or done those lines of coke. But the woman had had extra, what was he going to say, no?

"Get out of your place *now*." His contact's voice was urgent.

"What, why?"

"Uniforms are headed to pick you up for more questioning. Not sure why exactly but something is going down."

Panic detonated inside his chest, making it hard to breathe for a moment. "Your contact told you? Does he know you're warning me?"

The man snorted. "Hell no, he doesn't know. We were talking shop and about Taylor coming back to town to talk to the police. I made it sound like everyone at the office was worried about her—which they actually are."

He leaned against the wall outside his bedroom, his knees weak. "You're sure?"

"Yeah, it sounds like they've got some evidence that's going to clear her and implicate you. Get out now because if they bring you in…"

He wasn't ever getting out. That was the unspoken message. One he received loud and clear. "I'll be gone in less than two minutes. I'll contact you when I'm somewhere secure." He knew exactly where he was going but he sure as hell wasn't telling anyone else. Everyone could be bought or pressured.

"What do you want me to do about her? I'm still in Vegas and haven't been able to find her. I know she was in the hospital briefly, but I have no idea where she went when she left."

"Why was she in the hospital?" That didn't make sense unless he actually had winged her or maybe even shot her. But if he had, that had been a long damn time for her to wait to go to the hospital. He shouldn't have done that coke yesterday, but he'd needed it. It made everything in his life seem manageable. Damn it, had he missed something in the elevator?

"Don't know. Couldn't find out anything either."

Damn it. He hurried back into his room, still on his phone as he headed to his walk-in closet. The woman on the bed didn't stir. If he couldn't see the rise and fall of her chest he'd have thought she was dead. "And you haven't been able to track her through credit cards?"

The man snorted. "We wouldn't be having this conversation if I had. She's not using anything. And she's got backup of sorts. Not sure if it's that Vadim guy but whoever was at that house has some sort of training."

Neal knew his contact had never actually seen her at the house he'd gone to so it was possible she hadn't been there, but he'd bet she had been. Otherwise why had that man pulled a gun on his contact? It could have been because he didn't like people trespassing on his property. But from the account Neal had heard, his guy hadn't done anything to warrant a gun being pulled on him. And Neal believed him. He'd always come through before.

"Come back to town. If she's headed this way maybe you can cut her off before she makes it to the police station." He grabbed what he thought of as his run-bag, which was loaded up with extra clothes, toiletries and a small stash of cash. Not a lot, but enough that he could get out of the city and stay unnoticed for a while. He'd need more to get out of the country though. He'd also need to buy a new ID, maybe a couple fake ones so he could lose anyone trying to track him and pick up all the cash he had stashed around the city. It wasn't the police he was worried about as much as the Russians. A shiver snaked through him at the thought of what they'd do to him. Everyone knew the stories about how they tortured their victims, but Neal had actually seen someone brutalized once. It had been a warning of sorts by their enforcer. The scary fucker had wanted to make sure Neal knew what would happen to him if he crossed them.

"You still want her eliminated?"

He paused, thinking about his options. He needed her dead before she talked to the police. Although if they had evidence that he was lying then it wouldn't matter if she was dead. Still, he couldn't stand Taylor. She'd always looked at him as if she was better than him. She'd come from nothing, unlike him. And she thought she was better? "If possible, yes."

"I'll try to get her but if she's coming in to the police station they might give her an escort. I'm not going down for you."

Neal was well aware of that fact. His contact was only helping him for the money. "I'll call you soon." Hanging up, he pulled on a pair of slacks and a light-gray, wool pullover sweater. Getting out of his condo unseen wouldn't be hard. He had good security but there were a couple exits he could use to get out without any guards seeing him on camera. Since he didn't know when the police would be here, he wasn't going to waste time waking up the woman in his bed.

If anything, maybe the cops would waste time questioning her—whatever her name was—which would give him a better lead time. Not that he was leaving the city. Not yet. He needed more information, needed to know exactly what the police had on him. If he didn't have to flee, he didn't want to. He liked his name and the life he'd created. Not to mention running from the Russians was stupid. But if the cops had proof that he'd killed Hugh and tried to kill Taylor then he was gone. He'd be looking over his shoulder the rest of his life, but fuck, he'd just have to do it because he wasn't going in a cage.

Everything of importance he owned was in a storage locker, his safety deposit box, or on his boat. While he hated the thought of leaving his condo forever, there was nothing irreplaceable in it. Bag in hand, he grabbed his laptop and headed out. As he hurried to one of the stairwells, he pulled up his private bank account using his cell phone. When he couldn't login, he frowned and called the bank. There seemed to be something wrong with his pin. A slither of anxiety worked its way through his system.

By the time he'd made a safe exit and left on foot, using the connection to a neighboring condo complex to locate his extra getaway car, he was beyond raging. With the exception of ten fucking dollars, all the money in his account was gone.

Transferred. To who the fuck knew where.

There was no way to stop it either. His heart beat out of control, the pulsing in his ears so loud he felt as if he was going to split apart at the seams. This couldn't be happening.

Where had his money gone?

Taylor. That bitch must have taken it. Which meant he had no way to pay off the Russians.

She was too smart for her own good. Glancing around, he was thankful to see he was alone in the parking lot neighboring his condo. He wondered how long the cops would take to get there. Even with everything going on it made him laugh to think of how that woman in his bed would react to being woken up by cops. Too bad he wouldn't get to see it.

Once he made it to the older model Prius he'd paid for in cash months ago, he started the engine. But he didn't leave right away. The windows were tinted and he'd been sure to avoid all video surveillance when leaving out the side exit. He used his phone to check his work email, then half a dozen other work related accounts.

Locked out of all of them.

This was definitely Taylor's doing. His fingers tightened around the steering wheel as wave after wave of uncontrollable anger raged through him. She was dead no matter what happened. If he had to strangle the life out of her himself, he'd do it with no problem. No one stole from him and got away with it.

* * *

"You okay?" Roman asked quietly from the seat next to Taylor. He slid the pad of paper where he'd just finished his statement about yesterday's events onto Detective Hurley's desk.

They were sitting in Hurley's messy, small office. Unlike what she'd seen of police stations on television and from her experience as a teenager when her mom had taken her down to the police station to press charges against her stepfather, there were quiet offices on the second floor above the main first floor. Hurley had dropped them off here, given them paper to make their statement and said he'd be right back.

Taylor had already finished scribbling down what she knew about yesterday and refused to look at Roman, but nodded. "Yeah, I'm good." She could feel him drilling holes in her with that intense gaze of his, but she didn't care. She'd heard what he said about wanting to get rid of her. It hurt her more than she'd realized, especially after that kiss they'd shared.

Well screw him. She wanted to be gone too.

Wrapping her arms around her middle, she turned completely away from Roman, looking at a big bookshelf on one wall. Thick notebooks and what looked like procedural manuals were stacked on it. On the top shelf was a picture of Hurley wearing a football uniform and holding a helmet under his arm. "Did he play pro football or something?" It would certainly make sense considering how big he was.

"Nope," Hurley said, stepping into the room and making her nearly jump. Carrying a manila folder and a cup of what she assumed was coffee, he nodded at both of them. "I played in college, but got injured. I was never going to go pro anyway." She didn't hear any wistfulness in his voice and he continued quickly, not giving her a chance to respond. "I've got good news, bad news, and just news."

"Good news first," Roman murmured, sitting up at full alert, his body coiled tight, like a predator.

She hated that she was remembering what he looked like without his shirt on and how she'd felt with his big body pressing her down against his bed . . . Wait, Hurley was saying something. She snapped her gaze to where he sat behind his desk, his expression grim.

"The good news is that the bullet tested positive for your blood type," he said, looking at Taylor. "I guess Powers Group has that information on file?"

She nodded. "Yes. I travel a lot with Hugh—used to travel with him—sometimes internationally so they've got most employees' pertinent information in case there's ever a disaster."

"Until they do a DNA comparison they won't know for sure that it's you, but it's sure not Neal Lynch's type. Which brings me to the bad news. He's in the wind."

In the wind? "He's . . . gone?"

"Yeah," Hurley said, his mouth pulled into a tight line. They went to pick him up this morning and he was already gone. Doesn't look like much is missing, but a woman he'd brought home last night was there and had no idea he'd even left. They've run his cell phone records and he received a call from a burner phone about ten minutes before Oceanside PD showed up at his place. Now he's either ditched his phone or turned it off because they can't track him. Not the actions of an innocent man."

A heavy feeling settled in the pit of her stomach. Despite the hurtful words Roman had said earlier about her, she glanced at him. His expression was unreadable, but he reached out and squeezed her hand in silent support. She looked back at Hurley. "Timing of that phone call can't be a coincidence."

"Nope. And the call originated from somewhere in Vegas. So it could be the guy who came after you yesterday. My money's on it being him because I don't believe in coincidence."

Iciness settled over her as she tried to digest everything. Neal and whoever he'd hired to come after her were still out there.

"What are they doing to hunt him down?" Roman asked.

"They already got a warrant and have frozen all his assets so he doesn't have access to any money right now. He could have accounts we don't know about, but they're digging into all his records trying to find out if Lynch's got any extra houses or something that will lead them to him."

"What about the man who came after Taylor yesterday," Roman continued, his body language never changing.

"We're still looking for the guy, but so far we're coming up empty. There's just no evidence to go on. It's another reason for you," Hurley said, looking at Taylor, "to get back to California immediately. You need to make an official statement and lay low for a while. At least until Lynch is caught. And he will be. Without funds he's going to be fucked . . . uh, screwed. Once he's caught he'll turn on the guy he hired to come after you. A man like him has no loyalty. Is there a place you can go after you've made your statement?"

"Yeah, maybe," she murmured, the wheels in her head turning. She didn't even want to think that far ahead. She needed to talk to the Oceanside PD then figure out what to do about Hugh's funeral. After that she'd worry about everything else.

"How are you going to get back home? It'll take some time but considering the situation, I think we can arrange an escort—"

"I'm taking her," Roman interrupted.

She looked at him in surprise. "Um, that's not necessary. I'm sure you can't wait to get rid of me," she snapped with more heat than she'd intended. Gah, she hadn't wanted him to know he'd hurt her. Without waiting for his response, she turned back to Hurley. "I can either drive or Powers Group has a company jet. I can probably use it. I just . . . normally I'd talk to Benjamin Escobar—he's head of security there—but I don't know if I can trust him."

The detective's eyebrows raised slightly. "Why do you say that?"

She lifted her shoulders as Roman's phone started buzzing in his pocket. In the small room it was easy to hear. He pulled it out and glanced at the caller ID. His jaw clenched once before he met her gaze. "I've got to take this, but whether you take your company jet or not, I'm going with you." At that, he got up and left, his rubber-soled shoes silent as he entered the hall and moved out of sight.

Frowning, she turned back to Hurley. Taylor wasn't certain what she'd expected, but it wasn't that. She'd thought Roman had wanted her gone so why was he insisting on coming with her? Maybe he felt he owed it to Vadim. Shaking off the thought, she said, "Remember the man I told you about last night, Gordon Simpson?"

"The one waiting outside the PD?"

"Yeah. Escobar is his boss. I guess he could have been working for just Neal, but I don't know. Escobar is kinda scary. I don't see any of his guys doing something without him knowing." Which she knew made her sound like a little kid, but she didn't care. Benjamin Escobar had an edge to him.

Hurley snorted softly. "Well, scary or not, Escobar vouched for you. Went on record with the guys at Oceanside and said there was no way you killed Mr. Powers."

She straightened in her seat, surprise jolting through her. "He did?"

"Yep. I don't know for sure but it sounds like he's got a good relationship with the department there and he made sure the detectives on the case knew his thoughts about you."

"Oh." She bit her bottom lip, digesting the newest piece of information.

"I've already passed on the info about Simpson though so hopefully by the time you get back to Oceanside they'll know more about why he was at the station. If it had anything to do with you, they'll find out. Powers was an influential, powerful man. They're working around the clock to close the case."

"Good." That didn't mean she believed Escobar wasn't involved. But why would he have vouched for her to the police when he barely knew her? They'd worked at the same company for a while but he was not a warm, friendly type. That being an understatement.

She felt as if her brain was about to go into overload and she just hoped she could count on the man as an ally.

* * *

Roman didn't stray too far down the hall as he answered his phone. If it was anyone else, he'd have ignored the call, but when Wyatt Christiansen called, he answered.

"Hey, boss," he said quietly.

"Roman. What's going on with Taylor Arenas? Has she been arrested?" That was something he liked about the man. He always got right to the point.

"How do you even know about that?" And how did Wyatt know Taylor? His billionaire boss was happily married but that strange sense of possessiveness swept through Roman again nonetheless.

He snorted softly. "Vadim."

Roman wondered why Vadim had mentioned it to Wyatt at all. "She's fine and no, she's not being arrested. I'm taking her back to Oceanside in the next hour or so." Because no matter what she said, he wasn't letting her out of his sight. Ever since they'd left his house earlier, she'd been quiet, withdrawn. He'd thought maybe she regretted the kiss they'd shared but after what she'd said in Hurley's office about him wanting to be rid of her, he realized she'd heard what he said to his brother. Roman wanted to kick his own ass for saying that lie out loud. As soon as they were alone, he was going to explain to her why he'd said it.

"How are you getting there?"

Roman paused. He respected his boss, but his personal business was just that. Personal. And he was off for the next few days so it wasn't like this would interfere with his work schedule. Unless he was missing something here, Wyatt should have no reason to be asking about Taylor. "Respectfully, why do you want to know about Taylor?"

Wyatt let out a short sigh. "I've been trying to hire her away from Powers Group for years. Vadim's assured me she's innocent and I . . . I respected Hugh Powers. I just want to make sure Taylor's all right."

"More like you want to get a head start on the headhunting," he said dryly. The words were out before he could censor himself. He liked and respected his boss a lot, but he was always very aware of their professional relationship. Unlike Jay, Wyatt's right-hand man, Roman didn't have that type of relaxed relationship with the billionaire where he always said what was on his mind.

To his surprise, Wyatt let out a sharp laugh. "You're not totally wrong. She'd be a big asset to me if I could hire her, but Vadim asked me to help out."

And Vadim never asked for anything. Wyatt didn't say it, but Roman knew it was true and part of the man's reasoning. Vadim was a fucking genius and someone Wyatt would never want to lose. "Fair enough. I'm driving her back. Shouldn't take us more than five or six hours. And I'm taking her directly to the police station."

"You can take the private jet. I'll have Ellie set it up."

"I thought Ellie was off." Ellie was Wyatt's assistant but Roman was sure she'd taken off work with her new husband, Jay. He had friends in town who hadn't been able to make it to their wedding and Jay had wanted to show off his new wife. He hadn't said the words but Roman knew Jay well.

"Damn it, I forgot. I'll have her temp do it or I'll just do it myself," he grumbled and Roman figured he was counting down the seconds until the efficient blonde returned to work. "Just show up at the hangar when you can, I'll make sure you've got a ride." He disconnected before Roman could respond.

Not exactly surprising. When Wyatt was done talking, he was done talking and nothing else needed to be said.

The jet ride was a nice surprise, faster, and a whole lot more secure than him driving Taylor. He didn't think she'd have an issue flying considering she'd mentioned taking her company's jet, but he had a feeling she'd have an issue with him going. Not that it mattered, it was happening. Because he was making sure she made it to California safely and he wasn't trusting her safety to anyone but himself.

Taylor was more than just an obligation. It didn't matter that he hadn't known her long, he found that he wanted to know every little thing about this woman. And he wasn't letting her out of his sight.

CHAPTER EIGHT

Taylor gratefully took the bottle of water the flight attendant gave her and tried not to wonder what Roman was doing at the front of the plane. The tall, slender woman was beautiful and looked runway ready even in her blue and white uniform. Her inky-black hair was pulled up into a complicated-looking chignon and her lips were a ruby red that made the woman look like freaking Snow White.

Meanwhile Taylor was wearing borrowed clothes that didn't fit right, had no makeup on and was wearing her zombie heels. Okay, her heels were actually awesome and the only thing that made her feel better. But she felt like crap otherwise and the dull throbbing in her side wasn't helping any. And she really didn't like the flirty looks the flight attendant had been giving Roman when they'd first boarded. Even if she couldn't blame the woman.

It wasn't like Taylor had a claim on him and he didn't even want to be with her so whatever. His brother had taken them to the airport so she'd mainly talked to him, basically ignoring Roman. She'd felt as if he wanted to talk more to her, but she just couldn't deal with how he made her feel all manic. Shutting her eyes, she leaned back against the plush, leather seat and tried to relax even though it was impossible when she knew what was waiting for her at the end of the flight.

"What you heard me tell my brother was bullshit." Roman's voice startled her.

She hadn't even heard him approach. Opening her eyes, she turned in her seat to find herself staring into his mismatched eyes and fought that increasingly familiar sensation of being swallowed up by the man just by looking at him. "Excuse me?" As soon as they'd boarded he'd headed up to the cockpit and she hadn't seen him even during takeoff. It was clear he knew the pilot and co-pilot, probably from previous travel with his boss. A shockingly jealous part of her had wondered if he'd been on more than friendly terms previously with the flight attendant. Ugh, she didn't like feeling like this.

He sat directly next to her in one of the big, comfortable, leather seats instead of across the aisle from her, his nearness putting her on edge. That familiar masculine, woodsy scent wrapped around her as he leaned closer, his body heat scorching. "I don't want to get rid of you."

She wasn't going to pretend she hadn't heard him at his place, because his words had hurt. "Then why'd you say it? Are you embarrassed by me?" That insecure part of her she thought she'd left behind in high school flared to the surface. The girl who'd never quite fit in—and still felt awkward in a lot of social situations—and wondered why a man like Roman had even kissed her.

He blinked as if she'd truly surprised him, something she figured didn't happen too often. "Embarrassed? Why would I be embarrassed by you?"

His surprise soothed her ego, but she still wanted an answer to her first question. She shrugged. "Why'd you say it?"

He scrubbed a hand over his face. "I don't know."

"That's helpful," she muttered, annoyance ratcheting up more than hurt.

Gritting his teeth, he met her gaze. "That kiss took me off guard and . . . I don't fucking know. You make me feel crazy and I didn't want to deal with questions from my brother when I had no idea how to answer him."

Okay now she was confused. "I make you feel crazy?"

"Yeah." His voice dropped an octave and he leaned in a fraction before he stopped himself and pulled back. Not enough to put actual distance between them, his masculine scent teasing her senses as it wrapped around her. "I'm near you and I want to kiss you. I think about you, and I get fucking hard," he growled.

Her lips parted in surprise and just like that, his gaze dropped to her mouth and he let out a soft groan she might not have heard if they weren't sitting so close.

"Are you hard right now?" she whispered, unable to take her gaze from his face.

"As stone." His words were a guttural confession.

Just like that her nipples hardened and heat flooded between her legs. His words were like a full-body caress for how they affected her.

Unable to stop herself, her gaze dipped down but he had his laptop case placed over his lap. When she looked back at him, his gaze seemed to darken as he watched her intently, waiting for a response.

She leaned a fraction closer, as if drawn by the magnetic pull between them. "My nipples are hard too," she whispered, the bold admission unlike her. Everything going on in her life might be insane, but the attraction she felt for Roman probably took the cake. There was no explaining it.

"I'm not looking for a relationship," he quietly blurted.

Okay, that doused some of her desire, but . . . her gaze fell to his mouth again and her nipples tightened even harder against her bra cups. "Good. Neither am I." Which was mostly true. She didn't have time for a relationship, especially now, but that didn't mean she didn't want Roman. Maybe some good sex would be enough to get him out of her system. Though part of her was really disappointed by the no relationship statement even if she wasn't looking.

The flight attendant chose that moment to interrupt them, asking Roman if he needed anything else. He answered no without looking at her, which made Taylor smile. Once they were alone again, she leaned back against her seat and tried not to fantasize about going to bed with him. She felt guilty for her thoughts with everything else going in.

It was definitely time for a subject change. "How do you like working for Wyatt Christiansen?"

Roman paused for a long moment, as if he didn't like the shift in topic, but then he sighed and seemed to relax, the tension in his shoulders loosening as he leaned back against his seat. He was still turned in her direction. "He's a good boss. Benefits are good too. He takes care of his people."

"That's a very succinct answer."

His lips twitched as if he wanted to smile—she wondered what it would take for him to full-on smile at her. "There's not much else to say. The guy's a hard ass when he needs to be, but he's fair. I like working for him and I like the people I work with. Did he offer you a job again?"

Her eyebrows raised at his question. "You know he's offered before?"

"He mentioned it when he called earlier."

"He could have contacted me for all I know but I still don't have my phone." Or her laptop, her tablet, e-reader or half a dozen other electronic devices she was used to carrying with her at all times. Being so disconnected was jarring.

At the same time, it was also oddly nice not to have to deal with anyone who'd known Hugh, whether they thought she was guilty or not. The thought of talking to people she worked with about Hugh made her want to tailspin into a breakdown.

"I don't think he'd make an offer just yet." Roman's voice was dry.

Taylor snorted. "Yeah, but this jet is a nice touch. If it wasn't for Hugh I probably would have considered Mr. Christiansen's offer—well, offers." But she hadn't even thought about it, nice as it was to be headhunted. Now she had no clue what she planned to do once the dust settled. One of the main reasons she'd stayed with Powers Group was because of Hugh and because she loved her job. Now the thought of going back to work for the company was depressing.

Roman seemed to sense her mood change because he reached out and squeezed her hand. "We'll be there soon, rest if you want," he murmured.

She wished he wasn't being so sweet and caring. Okay, that wasn't true. She was incredibly appreciative of his support. It just made it harder because she knew this wasn't going to last. Throat tight with a cacophony of emotions brought on by thoughts of her dead friend, she nodded and closed her eyes. The seat was like a big cloud so it wasn't hard to relax. She couldn't help but notice that Roman never let her hand go.

And she wasn't inclined to pull it back from him. He made her feel safe, grounded and . . . not so alone.

***

"You ready?" Roman asked quietly as he and Taylor waited to disembark. As soon as they'd landed he'd received a call from Wyatt—who'd clearly taken a personal interest in this situation—letting him know that the detective assigned to the case, two uniformed officers and three men from Powers Group security were waiting for them. No one wanted to take any chances that Taylor didn't make it to the police station.

After watching a couple news clips on his phone before they'd taken off, he'd seen how much the media was paying attention to the story of Hugh Powers' death. No doubt the Oceanside PD wanted this wrapped up quickly and efficiently. There'd recently been an earthquake a couple hours north though so half the media attention was on the natural disaster.

Taylor nodded, her bright blue eyes seeming more vivid against her face under the afternoon sun streaming in through the open windows. "I think so. Guess it doesn't matter now . . . Thank you for coming with me."

He just grunted, not needing her thanks. Not wanting it. All he wanted to do was chase away the shadows in her eyes, see her smile. A real one.

When the plane door opened, she tensed next to him. Seconds later the pilot, co-pilot and flight attendant thanked them for flying with them with smiles on their faces—Wyatt's people were always professional—before Roman and Taylor exited.

Carryon bag in hand, he went first, wanting to shield her from everything. Two matching, black SUVs and a slightly smaller black Ford Explorer were on the tarmac not far from the plane. Six men in total waited at the bottom. Three in black suits with black ties. All alert, all armed even if he couldn't see their weapons. Two men were in police uniforms and one man was in slacks and a sports coat. He was the tallest. His hands were shoved in his pockets, pushing the bottom of his coat back and revealing his badge hooked on his belt. When he saw them, he straightened.

Roman reached behind him with his free hand and was pleased when Taylor took his hand. Moments later as they reached the bottom of the rolling stairs, the tallest man approached. Oh yeah, definitely the detective on the case.

The tall, lanky man with dark hair nodded at both of them, his focus narrowing on Taylor as he pushed his sunglasses back on his head. "Ms. Arenas?"

"You can call me Taylor," she said softly, clutching Roman's hand tightly as she came to stand next to him. He liked that she was leaning on him, but told himself not to get used to this.

"I'm Detective Durnin, but Byron is fine. You've been through quite an ordeal."

She nodded and Roman was getting to know her enough that he realized she didn't trust herself to speak.

"Yes, she has," Roman answered for her.

The detective looked at him, his expression guarded. "Are you her attorney?"

"No, I'm Roman MacNeil. I work for Wyatt Christiansen. Taylor is coming in of her own accord because she's done nothing wrong. But if at any time I deem necessary—if you try to steamroll her with bullshit—Mr. Christiansen's attorneys are on-call for her." There was a bite of warning to Roman's words. He wanted everyone to understand how they could and couldn't treat Taylor. He knew he was likely being an overprotective dick, but he didn't care. If someone had an agenda or wanted to make a name for themselves, sometimes innocent people got caught in the crossfire. In this situation he didn't think that would happen when the most viable suspect had disappeared, but he was covering all of Taylor's bases for now. She was a strong woman, but she was also emotionally connected to this case.

Next to him Taylor jerked slightly at his words. He hadn't told her what Wyatt had said, but it was true. If at any time Roman thought Taylor needed legal representation, he was supposed to call Wyatt's guy in case she didn't have an attorney of her own. And Roman doubted she could call the law firm who represented Powers Group because of the conflict of interest.

The detective's jaw tightened, but he simply nodded. "I'm aware of the situation." His expression softened a fraction as he turned back to Taylor. "We've reviewed the statement you made with the Vegas PD and we're sorry for your ordeal. Do you need medical attention before we head to the station?"

Taylor shook her head. "No, I'm okay. I just want to take care of all this now."

As soon as she'd spoken, one of the men in suits came forward, a broad-shouldered, stocky Hispanic man, his laser-like focus on Taylor.

Roman instantly tensed, taking a small step forward out of instinct even though it was clear the police knew who these men were or they wouldn't have been allowed on the tarmac.

"As agreed, she'll be riding there under our protection," the Hispanic man spoke as he nodded at Taylor.

Must be Benjamin Escobar. Wyatt had told Roman the man would be here.

The detective nodded and Roman could tell he wasn't a fan of the situation. But he guessed Durnin's higher-ups wanted this situation handled with kid gloves. A young, innocent woman had been shot then forced to go on the run because she'd been terrified the man who'd killed her boss would come after her—after the police had missed key evidence in the elevator.

"We'll be right behind you," the detective said before nodding at the two men in uniform and heading for the idling Explorer.

"I'm sorry about Hugh, Taylor," Escobar said as he motioned toward one of the SUVs. He sounded sincere, but the man was hard to read. If Roman had to guess, however, the guy had definite military training. It was in his bearing and vigilant posture. "The police are going to catch that fucker Neal."

"Thanks, Benjamin. I heard that you told the police I wasn't involved even before I came forward."

The man lifted his shoulders. "I knew you didn't do it. You loved him too much."

To Roman's surprise, Taylor started crying. Tears streamed down her cheeks and Escobar stared at her in horror, as if the sight of her tears was too much to handle. Roman understood the feeling.

"Sorry, just nice that someone actually believed me," she murmured, her voice watery as she leaned into Roman's outstretched arm.

Escobar didn't respond, just cleared his throat and looked away, clearly uncomfortable with the display of emotion.

Roman tugged her close, needing to comfort her as they reached one of the SUVs. The passenger door opened and when a blond man got out, Taylor immediately froze.

All of Roman's senses went on alert. Without thinking, he stepped in front of her and went to reach for a weapon that wasn't there. Because he traveled so much with Wyatt, he and all security personnel who worked for the billionaire were able to carry in multiple states. But this wasn't an official work thing so he'd kept his weapon packed and unloaded. Unarmed or not, he'd take this guy down if he posed a threat to Taylor.

Escobar let out a short sigh. "Taylor, I know your concerns with Simpson and they're unfounded. He was at the—"

"Taylor, I'm not working for or with Neal," the man said heatedly, but not with anger. Just concern. "I was at the police station yesterday waiting for my girlfriend to get off work. She's a dispatcher. We live together and her car is in the shop. I just didn't want her to have to catch a ride home." The guy had blond hair, but it wasn't the man who'd shot at Roman outside Vadim's house. Even though most of the guy's face had been obscured, he had a slightly smaller build and his voice was different. Didn't mean Roman was completely removing the guy from his radar.

"He's telling the truth, Taylor. He was with me most of yesterday at the office." It seemed as if Escobar wanted to say more, maybe really defend the guy, but didn't.

Taylor sidestepped Roman, but still hovered a little behind him. "Okay," she said, not much conviction in her voice.

They didn't have time for this and Roman didn't want Taylor around a man who clearly made her uncomfortable. "We need to get to the station and she's not riding with him." Roman knew he was being rude, but didn't care.

Seemingly unsurprised, Escobar nodded. "No problem. We'll take the other SUV."

It was clear Simpson wanted to say more and he actually appeared as if he felt bad, but Roman didn't care. No one was innocent or a non-threat as far as Taylor was concerned. Right now the only goal was to get her to the police station unharmed.

* * *

Neal stepped out of the small bathroom of his forty-foot cruiser. As boats went this was a decent sized one. Some called it a yacht, but to him, only cruisers over sixty feet should be designated with that title. While he might wish for something flashier and bigger—which he would get one day—for now this boat did its job of keeping him safe and under the radar.

No one knew he was here and he had enough food to last for a week without having to leave the marina. He'd chosen this particular one because it was mid-sized. Not so small that he would have regular neighbors who paid attention to him and not so large that he wouldn't see or hear if the police were coming for him. Or the Russians. That was key right now. He was still waiting to hear back from his contact who'd arrived back in town not long ago. The guy had said he might have news about Taylor.

All this waiting was making him fidgety. He needed something to take off the edge. When his phone buzzed across the built-in teak dresser of the master stateroom, he snapped it up.

It was a text from his contact. *She's on her way to the station.*

Stop her, he texted back furiously.

His phone buzzed again with a new message. *Cant. Protected. No way around it.*

That was annoyingly cryptic but Neal understood the need for it now. He still wasn't sure if the police had anything on him and he hadn't been able to check his personal bank accounts. He couldn't use his phone because if he did and the cops were onto him, they'd be tracking him. And if he logged on to an account they were watching, he was certain they'd be able to track him. As soon as he could sneak away, he'd be calling his regular bank and checking his funds there.

What do they know? he texted.

No news yet.

Damn it. He tapped his finger against the dresser for a moment, raw energy humming through him in jagged spikes of panic as he tried to think about his next move. He could ask his contact to check his accounts for him, but if he did that it could be bad for multiple reasons. Neal didn't want to risk giving his personal info to the man and if the accounts were being watched, he didn't want to reveal his link to his best source of help right now. He let out a savage curse and texted back. *Keep me updated.*

Fuck it. He should just cut and run. His gut told him to get out of town. He had a couple burners and could check his accounts from one of them or from a local coffee shop. They all had free Wi-Fi. Even if he was being tracked he'd be able to get in and out of a coffee shop in no time, especially in a crowded shopping area. Yes, that was exactly what he'd do.

Shoving his phone in his pocket, he grabbed his ball cap and ascended the short set of stairs from the stateroom into the galley.

And froze at the sight of the tattooed man leaning casually against the long, narrow island.

Neal swallowed hard, but pasted on a smile as he stepped into the brightly lit room. It attached to the living room and even with all the blinds drawn, there were so many windows that the afternoon light streamed through the cracks, illuminating everything. "Alexei, surprised to see you here." Neal wondered if that was even the Russian mob enforcer's name. The first time he'd met him had been six months ago. The man had said to call him Alexei, not that it was his actual name. Then he'd broken Neal's pinky and ring finger just because he could.

The man didn't move, just watched Neal with those creepy, green eyes that reminded him of a deadly predator. "You have a payment coming up." There was just the slightest accent in his voice, barely discernable, as if he was trying to lose it.

"Thursday, I know." Which was why he needed to make a decision fast. Stay or leave. It was Tuesday afternoon so there wasn't much time.

"Thinking of leaving town?"

He made a scoffing sound. "No."

"I hear your partner is dead and that you killed him."

Neal could feel the blood drain from his face. "What?"

"Hmm." The Russian made the non-committal sound as he reached for one of the knives in the Cuisinart knife block set on the island. Instead of pulling one out, he just ran a finger—a gloved one—along the row of handles. "We do not care about your problems. All my boss cares about is what you owe him. He has been very generous giving you a payment plan."

Neal had the irrational urge to snort in derision, but he wasn't suicidal. The plan was anything but generous. He was getting raped on the interest. The only reason the Russians had agreed to let him have a payment plan—because they did nothing without getting something.

"I'm here to let you know that if you go to prison, your debt is not erased. If you try to negate on your deal, you won't make it to prison. And if you try to run..." He trailed off, pinning him with that deadly gaze, and smiled. It was like looking at a great white shark smiling. "I don't enjoy many things about my job, but I will enjoy hurting you."

"Taylor Arenas stole my money," Neal blurted, immediately wondering if he'd just signed his own death warrant. Admitting he didn't have the cash was stupid, but if the Russians had found him here, he knew they'd find him if he ran. It was just a matter of time. Sure he had his boat, but that was part of Neal's backup plan if he had to go on the run. He couldn't offer it up to the Russians.

The man brushed an imaginary piece of lint off his black, leather jacket. The guy always wore black, like the grim fucking reaper. Probably because blood wouldn't show up on the color as well. The thought made Neal start to shake, but he tried to hide it and crossed his arms over his chest.

"That concerns me how?" Alexei sounded bored.

"The money I'd earmarked for your boss . . . She stole it."

The Russian shrugged. "You owe us. Not her. And it's not my problem if you can't hold on to your money. You have less than two days. Bring the cash by noon. You know the place. If you can't make the drop, just kill yourself. Don't make me chase you. Oh, I wouldn't go back to your place if I were you. The police are watching it." Without another glance, the man left, barely making a sound.

As soon as the enforcer was gone, Neal clutched the island counter with both hands, using it for support as he dragged in a long breath. If the Russians knew the police were after him they obviously had a contact, or more likely multiple contacts, in the police department. And if the cops were definitely watching his place, Neal was absolutely fucked. They wanted him for questioning because they had something on him—knew he was guilty. They wouldn't waste resources otherwise.

Unless he could get that money back. If he could get it back, he could pay off the Russians and disappear. Not his original plan, but he was willing to adapt. Because he couldn't look over his shoulder every night waiting for Alexei or someone like him to jump out of the shadows and slice him to ribbons. The man would make him suffer for days, weeks, make him eat his own dick. Neal had heard the rumors of his viciousness and didn't want to end up on the receiving end of Alexei's wrath.

His only option was to go after Taylor himself, terrify her enough that he forced her into giving him his money back. He didn't mind exacting revenge against her. Not at all. The thought of hurting her, making her suffer, was just icing on the cake.

Yes, he would get the money one way or another.

CHAPTER NINE

"My brain hurts," Taylor muttered from her seat next to Roman. They were in the back seat of one of the Powers Group's SUV's with Escobar driving them.

Roman didn't blame her. After spending the last few hours at the police station with Detective Durnin, he knew she had to be exhausted. "We don't have to go to Powers Group. I'm sure someone can bring you all your stuff," he murmured. It was going to be hard for her to go there, something he wasn't sure she fully realized.

"He's right. This isn't necessary," Escobar agreed.

Taylor shook her head once, the stubborn set of her jaw making it clear she was doing what she wanted. "No. I want to."

Roman leaned back against the seat and didn't push her. Taylor needed her cell phone and other belongings left in her car at the company parking garage but he had a feeling she wanted to go to her place of employment for another reason. Maybe to face it after what had happened, he wasn't sure.

They hadn't had any privacy since heading to the police station. He'd waited there with her while she answered questions—sometimes the same ones over and over—then filled out her official report. They'd also taken pictures of her wound and added it to the file the hospital in Vegas had sent over and the bloody clothes she'd given them. He'd insisted on changing her bandage and had made sure she took her antibiotics.

He found he liked taking care of her, looking out for her. Her words from earlier, that she wasn't looking for anything serious, kept playing in his head all day. Annoying the shit out of him. He *knew* he should be fucking thrilled she didn't want anything serious. But the knowledge rankled him in a way he didn't understand.

Unable to stop himself, his gaze strayed to her profile, drinking her in like a man dying of thirst. She'd pulled her long, dark hair into a ponytail. It was mostly straight but there were a few natural waves to it that gave her a sexy, just-got-back-from-the-beach look. Her blue eyes seemed even brighter in the interior of the SUV, shocking against her bronze skin. Skin he wanted to stroke his fingers and tongue over, nibbling on her jaw, kissing his way down the long column of her neck, before burying his face between her breasts. The shirt his brother had given her had a V-neck and even though she was petite, the woman was top heavy.

Something he could definitely appreciate.

Taylor delicately cleared her throat, making him jerk his gaze upward. Her lips twitched as she raised one of her eyebrows.

He shrugged unapologetically and reached for her hand, linking his fingers through hers. He didn't care that she'd caught him checking her out. Soon he planned to check out every inch of her naked body—and actually appreciate it while she wasn't passed out and injured.

"The building's mostly empty," Escobar said, his voice making both of them divert their attention to the front.

Roman bent down and looked through the windshield at the partially lit building they were approaching. Ten stories, Taylor had told him. "What's the security like?"

"We're on virtual lockdown, all the exits secured. All keycards have been deactivated for the night. If there's an emergency anyone can call me and gain access, but with everything going on, I didn't want anyone coming in late or Neal somehow gaining access through someone else's card."

Taylor straightened next to Roman, her body pulling taut. "Why would he want access to the building?"

Escobar shrugged and shot them a glance in the rearview mirror as he pulled up to a closed gate for the parking garage. "Any number of reasons. There are two uniformed police officers in the building doing a methodical search looking for any evidence of the weapon used to . . . the weapon used. When Neal was tested for GSR he had some on his clothing, but there wasn't the spray of blowback one would associate with recently firing a weapon. Which tells me he changed clothes and probably took a shower. Unless he managed to get the evidence out of the building before the cops showed up—and the timeline of Hugh's death and the entry/exit logs from our system don't allow for it—then he had to have stashed the clothes somewhere inside."

"But he's guilty, the cops seemed pretty sure of that." A tremor threaded through Taylor's voice, making Roman want to wring Neal Lynch's neck.

"Yeah, there's no doubt he is." Escobar rolled down his window and punched a code into the keypad before the gate raised.

On instinct, Roman glanced behind them again. He'd been scanning their surroundings since they'd left the PD. They still had an escort behind them, with three Powers Group Security guys, but Roman didn't know them and he didn't trust anyone where Taylor's safety was concerned. Except maybe Escobar. From what he'd seen of the guy, he liked him. More importantly, the man moved like he was trained. And the local PD trusted him. Roman planned to check him out more thoroughly, but his internal alarm wasn't going off around this guy and that counted for a hell of a lot. He always trusted his instinct.

"But," the man continued as he steered into the garage, "I wouldn't put it past that bastard to try anything for his defense. With your testimony, if it even goes to trial, and the evidence, it's pretty much a closed case, but they don't want to give him any room for a defense. If the weapon and his clothes are found, I doubt it'll even go to trial. It wouldn't make sense for him when he could take a deal."

"A deal?" Now she just sounded pissed.

Escobar snorted. "Yeah, a deal as in pleading down to a hundred years over a couple hundred. Once he's caught he won't see the outside of a prison again. Hugh had way too many powerful friends and Neal is going to burn."

"Good. Hey, where did Hugh's SUV come from?" Taylor asked suddenly before her eyes went wide.

Roman stiffened next to her. He knew she'd taken the SUV but hadn't told the cops she'd ditched it. She'd more or less avoided that topic and they'd been more concerned with the shooting and finding Neal than anything else. Arresting him was their top priority now.

Escobar snorted. "I know Hugh disabled all his GPS locators but I've got trackers on all company vehicles. He didn't like it, but he didn't have much choice because part of my job is to keep all executives safe. Man, I'm going to miss him," the head of security muttered before pulling into an empty parking space.

"Me too," Taylor said quietly, her fingers tightening in Roman's. "When's the . . . funeral? I didn't want to ask at the police station."

"Saturday. And I've taken care of everything. You'll need to talk to his attorney about some stuff he left you and there will be a shitload of things to deal with here, but I figured the least I could do was plan his funeral. He had pretty specific instructions." He turned off the engine and sat there for a moment. "How'd you get out of the city anyway?"

Now it was Taylor's turn to snort. "None of your concern. Thank you for taking care of everything, but let me know what I can do. I want to help."

He swiveled in the seat to look at both of them. "You can take some time off. Two weeks at least."

Roman liked that assessment. Taylor had been through a lot and whether she realized it or not, seeing that kind of violence up close and personal would have an effect on her. Maybe not right away but it would eventually.

"I'm not—"

"You are, and I'm not asking. According to the by-laws I'm the interim CEO with Neal and Hugh gone. At least until they can restructure. Now come on, let's get your stuff and get you out of here." He was out of the vehicle and had shut the driver's door before Taylor could respond with more than a sputter of indignation.

"Can you believe that?" she snapped, more to herself than Roman, he was sure.

Even though Roman agreed with Escobar, he kept his mouth shut. "Let's get your stuff then get out of here. I want to see you naked again."

She sucked in a sharp breath and looked at him, full-on, not the half-glances she'd been giving him since they'd gotten off the plane and had been dealing with the police all day. "What?"

"I want to bury my face between your legs and eat you out until you pass out from sheer exhaustion." The words were blunt and he got the exact response he'd been hoping for.

Her cheeks flamed crimson and she stared at him wide-eyed, all traces of her annoyance at Escobar and the situation gone. Her breathing had kicked up a notch and her pupils were dilated as she watched him. Oh yeah, she liked that idea a lot.

Which was good because he'd been thinking about it all damn day. Actually he'd been thinking about it since pretty much the moment she'd tried to knock him in the head with that vodka bottle.

"I know what you're doing," she finally murmured. "Trying to distract me."

He lifted one shoulder. "Distract you with the truth."

She blinked, sucking in another deep breath. Then she leaned in, almost as if she couldn't help herself, before stopping and pulling back. "Let's get this over with then you better make good on that promise."

Heat surged through him at her response, but he didn't answer. It was taking all his control to keep a tight lid on his lust for her. He opened his door and got out first, surveying the company's security group. According to Escobar they all had military experience and had been with the company for at least three years. Escobar trusted them but that didn't mean Roman had to.

"Your car hasn't been touched," Escobar said, nodding at the two-door car a few spots down.

"Really?" The surprise in Taylor's voice mirrored Roman's thoughts.

The man shrugged. "It wasn't part of the crime scene and personally," he looked over their shoulder to where the other men stood before lowering his voice a fraction, "I think the cops here did a shitty job until Detective Durnin took over. They did comb over your office though, but didn't take anything."

Her mouth pulled into a thin line as she shook her head. "Because there's nothing to take," she muttered as she headed to her car and opened the driver's side door.

"She needs extra security for tonight—at least," Roman said quietly to the other man. They were heading back to her place after this stop so she could pack up her clothes and whatever else she needed. Escobar had already arranged for her to stay at one of the company's executive condos—under a false name.

Tomorrow Roman planned to find somewhere else for Taylor to stay other than the condo, but for a few hours tonight it would do. With Neal gone and the man who'd shot at him still unknown, he wanted her somewhere completely unrelated to Powers Group.

Escobar nodded. "I know. The building itself is secure but I'll send you all the schematics. And I've got a four-man team I trust who will be standing guard directly outside the condo and in the lobby. None of them have ever worked directly with Lynch," he added, as Roman was about to ask for their resumes. "This is a big company, but these are my most trusted guys. They're all pissed about Hugh. And, as a precaution, none of them have the access code to get into the condo either. You'll be able to change it once you're both inside so that not even I know it. If someone breaches it, the police will be contacted immediately."

Escobar had already told him that Lynch actually knew about the condo, but it was secure—all of the company owned condos had been built with security in mind—and as long as he didn't have the access code, it was safer than a hotel or Taylor's place. Plus Lynch would have no reason to suspect she'd be staying there.

"Can you send me the files—just employee pictures and names—of any of your guys not working the last twenty-four to forty-eight hours?" Roman knew it was a big request and Escobar didn't owe him anything but he had to ask.

The man's eyes narrowed a fraction. "You think one of my guys came after her?"

"It's stupid not to consider the possibility. At least let me eliminate your guys by looking at their pictures." Because there was a high likelihood that Neal used easy resources and that included Powers Group security. It made more sense to look at the most obvious possibilities and while the man at Vadim's house had been wearing sunglasses and a hat, Roman wanted to try to identify him or at least narrow down the suspects. If he could give a list of names to Escobar or Taylor, they should be able to look at finances or anything else linking the shooter to Lynch. And if they couldn't, Roman knew Vadim could.

Escobar's jaw tightened, but he semi-relaxed as Taylor returned from her car, seemingly mollified by what she'd found. "All my stuff is there."

"Good," Escobar said, then nodded at Roman. "By the time you get settled in tonight, it'll be in your inbox."

He nodded back once. "Thanks."

"What will be?" Taylor asked.

"Just some files. I'll tell you on the way to your place," he murmured, glancing over his shoulder. They were still enough out of ear shot from the other men but he didn't want to talk about any of it until they were alone.

She looked as if she wanted to argue, but simply nodded. "Okay. I . . . need to grab some stuff from my office. Would you mind helping move our bags from the SUV to my car before we head up? It hurts a little to lift stuff."

Roman's eyebrows pulled together. "Your car's staying here. We're getting a ride to your place, then the condo. Tomorrow we'll figure out something else for transportation."

"We have a company vehicle you can use," Escobar interjected.

"I can't even drive my car?" She seemed surprised, or more likely she was just exhausted and not thinking about the situation with the same type of attitude Roman and the other man were.

He shook his head and reached out for her, needing to touch her. Even though he wasn't used to showing public displays of affection, he didn't care as he gently cupped her cheek. She instantly leaned into his touch. "It's safer if it stays here. With Lynch and the shooter out there, we don't need to give them any way to track you." Pulling Taylor close, he shot Escobar a look. "We'll take one of the vehicles tonight but tomorrow we're getting something else." Because Roman was taking more control of the situation and that meant making sure that wherever he went with Taylor, she wasn't being tracked by anyone.

"Fine. And whatever you need from your office, one of the guys can grab," Escobar said.

Taylor stiffened slightly against Roman. He looked down to find her biting her bottom lip, her expression unreadable. "I don't actually need anything from my office. I just . . . I thought maybe..." She trailed off and swallowed hard.

"You thought you might want to see where it happened?" he asked, purely guessing.

When her eyes filled with tears and she nodded, he let out a curse and pulled her into his arms. She buried her face against his chest, her petite body trembling against him. God, he was surprised she'd held up so well. It was too soon for her to see where Powers had been killed and he knew from experience that seeing the scene where her friend had died wouldn't do her a bit of good. But it wasn't his place to tell her. He might be domineering and used to taking charge of most situations, but he wouldn't right now. Not with this.

"No one's allowed up there now," Escobar said quietly. "It's marked off with police tape."

Taylor shuddered as she sniffled and stepped back. Roman kept his arm protectively around her as she turned back to face Escobar, wiping at her eyes. "That's probably for the best."

Roman kissed the top of her head. "It is. Now let's get out of here so I can take care of you." Words he'd never said to any woman.

Nodding, she tucked into his hold as he led her back to the SUV.

One of the other men called out to Escobar, telling him they'd be the lead vehicle and had her address plugged into their GPS. Once Escobar, Taylor and Roman were back in the SUV, some of Roman's stress lessened. He didn't like Taylor being so exposed even in the relative safety of the vehicle.

Hell, he didn't like any of this. And he didn't know what to do with the strange protectiveness that welled up inside him whenever she was near. Since that had been practically the last thirty-six hours and it hadn't abated, he wasn't sure what the hell to do with his emotions. It was like she'd triggered something inside him and now that it had woken up, it sure as hell wasn't going away. He'd never felt like this, not even with his only serious ex. That relationship had been all about sex, something he could now see clearly. Because hindsight was a fucking bitch.

As Escobar steered toward the exit, he murmured something, clearly talking into an earpiece as they pulled out of the parking garage. When he turned onto the nearly deserted street, Roman automatically scanned their surroundings. Though there were signs for street parking, both sides were nearly empty except for two vehicles to the left of them. A truck and an SUV. No one was on either sidewalk, this part of town basically shut down after business hours.

"It should only take us about ten minutes to get to my place from here," Taylor said quietly, turning her body into Roman's so she was tucked up against his side.

Before he could respond a sudden barrage of pinging rained down around them, like rain on a tin roof. The staccato was an unfortunately familiar sound.

Shit. A punch of adrenaline shot through his system. *They were under attack.*

Taylor jerked and looked up in alarm, started to say something, but he grabbed her by the waist and shoved her to the floorboards in between the front and back seats, throwing his body on top of hers.

Escobar cursed and hit the gas, making the SUV fishtail as they sped away.

CHAPTER TEN

"The SUV's bullet resistant!" Escobar shouted from the driver's seat as the vehicle jerked forward, tires screeching as he made a sharp turn.

Adrenaline jagged through Taylor as she lay on the floorboards under Roman. He was turned away from her, looking toward the front seat, his profile grim.

Ping, ping, ping.

She cringed as more bullets slammed into the SUV. At first she'd been so confused when Roman had manhandled her to the ground. It had all happened so fast. Then she'd realized someone was *shooting* at them, and she was seriously close to having a full-blown panic attack.

When she watched movies that depicted women running around and screaming for no reason she always wanted to throw something at the screen. Or shake the women. She'd always wondered why on earth people screamed when the shouting couldn't do any good. Now she completely understood. And the only reason she wasn't screaming was because her throat felt as if it had swelled shut in pure fear. So she wasn't any better than those characters on television she'd always thought were ditzy. If her throat loosened just a bit, she was going to start having a massive, very loud breakdown of epic proportions. There was only so much she could take and she wasn't prepared for being shot at—again.

Escobar was saying something up front. Not to Roman though. Into his earpiece, she belatedly realized. He was ordering one of his guys to call the cops and telling them he was getting Roman and Taylor the hell out of there.

That was fine with her because she definitely didn't relish the idea of sticking around and facing a madman—or multiple crazies—with guns.

"Taylor!" Roman shouted.

She blinked and focused on his concerned face above her. By his expression she figured he'd said her name more than once. The shooting had stopped! Even though her ears were still buzzing, they weren't under fire. For now at least.

She slightly shook her head, trying to regain focus even though her insides were quaking like she was made of Jell-O. "Who was shooting at us? Are they still after us?" And her voice shook too, the questions coming out all high-pitched and screechy even as she tried to remain calm. Yeah, that wasn't working for her so well.

"Shooter unknown and no one is tailing us," Escobar said from the front, his voice clipped, as Roman pushed off her and went to help her up.

"I'm good here," she muttered, feeling too shaky to move. She didn't care if she looked crazy, she was safer down here. She wanted to drag Roman back down with her.

Roman's expression softened as he looked at her. He reached a hand down to her. "No one's following us, I swear."

The completely shaken part of her wanted to stay exactly where she was, but she took his strong hand and let him pull her up beside him. He almost, but not quite, pulled her into his lap. Murmuring words that didn't really sound like words, more or less just noises, he rubbed her back up and down as she turned into him. She'd always thought she'd be a lot stronger in a situation like this. Of course she'd never anticipated a situation where she'd be shot at multiple times in less than two days. Or ever, really.

"Benjamin, can you have one of your guys get Taylor's stuff from her place? She can give him a list of what she needs. I don't want to make another stop. If the cops need to talk to us, they can meet us at the condo. We're not waiting around anywhere." Roman phrased the first part as a question but it was pretty clear he wasn't asking.

Taylor pulled back at his words. She didn't want some random men going through her stuff. But one look at Roman's face and having the reality of the situation crash over her, she nodded and looked up at Escobar who flicked her a glance in the rearview mirror. "Yeah, I can tell them what to get," she muttered, realizing she probably sounded ungrateful. But she didn't have any energy left for niceties. She just wanted to get somewhere safe and crash into the sweet oblivion of sleep.

* * *

Taylor slipped on the plush, royal blue robe the company provided for all executives as she got out of the shower. Sighing, she loosely belted it around herself, careful of her wound, which barely bothered her now. She might just keep the robe when they left. Compensation for all her mental stress.

After combing her hair and doing a half-ass job of drying it, she smoothed some of the provided lotion on her newly shaved legs and let out a sigh of relief. Her aunt Esther had always told her that there wasn't much that a hot shower and a hot cup of tea couldn't cure. Or at least soothe. The sweet woman who'd been the only mother-figure Taylor ever knew, had been right.

The simple shower had done wonders for Taylor's outlook. At least she wasn't ready to spiral into a breakdown anymore. As long as no one shot at them for the rest of the evening—well day, considering it was after midnight—she'd be fine.

She rolled her shoulders as she stepped out into the large bedroom. Roman had given her the big bedroom but she was pretty sure they'd be sharing a bed later. Even if they didn't have sex, she was big enough to admit she didn't want to sleep alone. The color scheme of the huge room was dark blue, light gray and pearly white. The rest of the place was the same. Neutral, soothing to the eye—bland, like a hotel. The setup of the place was simple. Two huge rooms, both with ocean views, were separated by a living room with an entertainment center most men would probably drool over. The living room also had an ocean view, but they'd pulled all the drapes shut. The glass doors were all secured and bullet resistant because Powers Group didn't mess around with their visiting clients' security. While she didn't think someone from a boat or helicopter would be spying on them with binoculars, she still didn't like the idea of feeling so exposed.

For all she knew Neal could be on the beach watching. Unlikely considering Escobar had called in another security team and two of those guys were patrolling the strip of beach in front of the building. The extra security made her feel a lot better, but Roman's presence was the only thing helping her keep it together. She still couldn't believe someone had opened fire on them gang-style. It had been an actual drive-by, something that felt surreal to even think about.

When she stepped out of the bedroom into the tiled living room, she jerked to a halt.

Her stuff had been delivered while she'd been in the shower and Roman was going through her suitcase, which he'd opened up onto the thick, wood coffee table. "Uh, hello?"

He glanced up at her and half-smiled, but didn't stop what he was doing. "Hey, how was the shower?"

"Good . . . If you wanted to see my panties all you had to do was ask." She snatched a pair of boy-short Wonder Woman panties she was mortified one of the security team had grabbed. Balling it into her hand, she shoved it into one of the robe's pockets.

Roman snorted and spared her a quick glance. "I'm definitely seeing you in those later . . . And I'm just searching for any tracking devices. I know it's paranoid, but..." He trailed off, shrugging as he continued his methodical examination.

Paranoid, maybe, but she didn't mind in the least. They'd be leaving this place after they'd slept a few hours and she'd rather him take every precaution available. Because the truth was, she hadn't even thought about tracking devices. It seemed insane, but then Neal Lynch was clearly not right in the head. She still didn't understand why he'd opened fire on them. Or she assumed it was him who'd done it. It could have been the man he'd hired. Either way he'd clearly been willing to kill her and innocent men. She'd already made her statement to the police though and if she never had to make another report again that was fine with her. Maybe Neal thought with her dead he'd have a better defense—even though that sounded stupid.

"I'm going to make some hot tea. Do you want any?" she asked. When they'd arrived she'd scoured the cabinets and was grateful there were plenty of tea choices.

He shook his head as he ran his hand along the lining of her suitcase. "I'm good, but thanks."

Since he was intent on his task, she headed for the kitchen and made a pot of peppermint tea. The microwave would have been easier, but it felt wrong on so many levels to make tea that way. As she waited, she slipped her Wonder Woman panties on. Wearing nothing under the robe felt weird and she kind of hoped he'd been serious about seeing her in them later. Once the teapot whistled on the stove, she inhaled the familiar scent, letting it ground her before pouring herself a mug.

She found Roman still meticulously looking over her things. Considering what a private person she was, it was one of the first signs that this man had already gotten under her skin when she hadn't been paying attention. She wasn't sure if that was a good thing or not.

Bent over the table, searching her suitcase, his arm muscles flexed, his expression intense and insanely sexy. She could watch him all night but forced herself to do something productive. She pulled her laptop from the bag they'd retrieved from her car and turned it on. "Did you search my backpack?" she asked.

"Yeah, scanned your laptop first. It's clean."

Good. If Neal thought he was going to get away with any of this, especially the attack that could have hurt Roman, he was about to get a taste of her wrath. Sitting on the couch, she propped her feet on the coffee table and got to work.

"What're you doing?" Roman asked almost absently as he slipped one of his big hands into a zippered compartment, feeling around inside.

"Now that I've got a lot of Neal's information and complete access to his files, I'm going to start searching for him using it. It's very hard to go completely off the grid unless you use a new identity. Which he might very well have. But I'm not going to let him just get away without trying to track him down." She opened up a folder in one of his email accounts, scanning old messages. Investigations could be tedious work, but she was used to it and right now she was more determined than she'd ever been to dig up information on someone. And after she plugged in some key search words, she should be able to narrow down the right files quicker.

"You should leave that to the police." She could hear the frown in Roman's voice without looking at him.

"The police missed a key piece of evidence in this investigation. Not to mention…" She trailed off, wondering how much she should tell him about her past. Oversharing too soon was one of those relationship no-no's. Of course they weren't in a relationship.

"What?" he pressed.

Because she didn't want to see his expression when she told him, she kept typing in commands as she continued. "My stepfather was a cop. He killed my mom in a drunken rage." The words sounded almost robotic even though saying them felt as if she was being torn to ribbons on the inside. It was just too hard to let emotion seep through when she discussed it. She was already at a breaking point after everything that had happened the last couple days and didn't want to unleash too many long-buried feelings now.

She watched Roman still his movements out of the corner of her eye. He moved slowly and rounded the coffee table and sat next to her on the couch, still giving her some space. When he reached out and placed a gentle but possessive hand on the back of her neck, she tore her gaze from the laptop and looked at him. He watched her carefully but didn't say anything, obviously letting her talk when and if she wanted.

She'd never told any of the men she'd dated about her mom, had seen no reason to. But she wanted Roman to know this about her. Even if things between them never amounted to anything, she wanted him to know. "My mom was . . . everyone said she was a sweet woman. The truth was, she was weak. I've felt guilty for a long time because of the way I viewed her and I know it's hard for anyone being abused to leave their abuser, but she had *me*. Her daughter to worry about. And she tried a couple times to leave him, even went so far as to attempt pressing charges, but each time she was talked out of it because she could potentially ruin her husband's career." Taylor rolled her eyes at that, biting back the anger that surged through her any time she thought of that man.

"He eventually killed her in a drunken rage, jealous because he'd thought she'd been flirting with one of my teachers during a parent-teacher conference. He was always getting jealous about something and it was *always* stupid reasons. This time wasn't any different from the others, not at first anyway. But he started ranting and raving about how she didn't love him enough to give him a child of his own and just full-on freaking out. I'd always been pretty invisible to him, someone he had to deal with because I was my mom's daughter. That night . . . he looked at me differently. Like he wanted to kill me. I saw it in his eyes and my mom must have too. I didn't realize it until later, but she started provoking him, turning all his rage back onto her by admitting that she'd been flirting—when she hadn't. Then she screamed at me to leave and . . . I did. I ran to a neighbor's for help. By the time the police showed up it was too late. She was dead and he committed suicide by cop. Even at the end he was too weak to just kill himself." Her voice broke and she was surprised she'd been able to get it all out.

Roman's expression softened so much, it nearly shredded her. "Honey," he murmured, taking her laptop and putting it on the coffee table before pulling her into his lap.

She went willingly, savoring his comforting embrace as she laid her head on his shoulder. "I hated her for a long time, hated that she wasn't strong enough to leave him, that I wasn't enough of a reason for her to get away. I eventually realized that it had nothing to do with me. The aftermath of everything that happened, the way the cops acted as if his murderous rampage was a big shock to the community enraged me. To say it left a bad taste in my mouth where law enforcement is concerned is an understatement. I get that the majority of people in law enforcement are good and care about the people in their community—intellectually. But some days, like this Monday, all those buried feelings clawed their way to the surface, terrifying me."

His eyebrows drew together and he reached up with his hand, cupping her cheek and jaw, stroking over her skin with his thumb. The roughness of his thumb sent a shiver rolling through her. "No wonder you ran straight to Vadim's."

She shrugged. "In hindsight I probably could have handled things better but . . . it was like that sixteen year old just took over and escaping was all I could focus on."

"A sixteen year old with the ability to steal cars." His voice was wryly amused.

She laughed at the statement, the light humor taking her off guard and exactly what she needed. She didn't want to throw a pity party for herself or take a long trip down memory lane. She'd just wanted Roman to understand why she wasn't letting this go, why she wouldn't just sit back and let the cops take over. Obviously she wouldn't get in anyone's way but if she could find something for them to use, she would do it. "When I moved in with my aunt, one of the neighborhood boys taught me how to pick locks and steal cars among other things. I think he wanted to impress me."

"Such a bad girl," he murmured, the sudden drop in his voice sending a rush of heat between her legs. His tone and the heat in his eyes were so blatant she felt it all the way to her toes.

"And you were probably a boy scout."

His lips twitched up, but he didn't respond as his hand left her cheek and dipped between the lapels of her robe. She sucked in a breath as his big palm settled over one of her breasts, cupping it gently.

He kept his gaze pinned to hers as he oh-so-slowly rubbed this thumb over her already hardening nipple, sending shards of sensation cascading through her. "You wearing those Wonder Woman panties?"

She nodded, her eyes going heavy-lidded as he tweaked the nipple between his thumb and forefinger. "Want to see?" Surprised she'd even been able to find her voice, she grinned when his eyes went molten.

Wordlessly he slid her off his lap so that she was sitting on the couch. She spread her legs when he knelt in front of her, wondering what he planned. He'd told her exactly what he wanted earlier but she wasn't sure if he'd been serious. She really, *desperately* hoped he was.

He tugged the soft belt free before pushing the robe off her shoulders. It pooled down around her waist as her breasts and torso were exposed. When he fully parted the bottom part of it, spreading it open so that all of her was bared to him, she felt the strongest sense of power as he raked a hungry gaze over her. His lips twitched again in that adorable way of his when they landed on her undergarments. She had a lot of lace and silk but she preferred her boy-short style panties and was glad he liked them too.

He hooked his fingers under the elastic of them. "Lift up," he ordered softly.

Not needing to be told twice, she did. He slowly pulled them down her legs, tossing them behind him. If she'd thought he looked hungry before, it was a whole different story when she was fully bared to him.

He lifted one of her already spread legs by the ankle and kissed her inner calf. She felt incredibly exposed, heat flooding between her thighs and her nipples tightening to almost painful points at the sensation of being so exposed to him. Her lower abdomen tightened as he held her leg like that, kissing her and watching her intermittently. As if he wanted to see her every reaction.

Slowly, he made his way up her leg, raking his teeth over her skin then following up with little nibbles and kisses.

She slid her fingers through his short, buzzed hair. It wasn't long enough to grab onto so she just clutched his head. When he reached her upper inner thigh, he leaned into the juncture of her thighs and inhaled deeply.

Her face flamed at what he was doing. It was such a raw, sexual act. Then he shuddered, his big body just trembling in a way that turned her on even more. As he'd been kissing his way up her body she'd felt nervous, almost weird about being so exposed like this, but at his reaction something shifted inside her.

She might be naked and in a vulnerable position, but something told her she had all the power right now.

Shifting slightly, he kept one hand pressing her thigh open then leaned down and peppered kisses over her lower abdomen, right above her mound. *Teasing her.* His breath was warm against her skin as he blazed a hot path just over her most sensitive area.

Her inner walls clenched and she tightened her fingers against his head. "Are you seeing how long you can tease me?" she whispered, her voice raspy, and really wishing he was just as naked as she was. She wanted to see every inch of him right now.

He chuckled against her, but didn't look up as he turned his head and grazed his teeth over the section of skin where her inner thigh met her—oh! He moved suddenly, sucking on her clit and she nearly vaulted off the couch.

"Roman," she cried out.

In response, he dipped his tongue inside her and she lost any semblance of controlling herself that she might have had. He held onto one of her ankles and lifted it up to the couch so that her heel was on the edge. The position kept her wide open for him.

She didn't need him to keep her leg in place, but she liked the feel of him holding her there as his tongue dipped inside her again.

Stroking, stroking, *stroking*, and making her insane as she writhed against him. He shifted positions again and moved back to her clit, the pulsing bundle of nerves begging for his kisses. It was too much and not enough as he zeroed in on her, his rhythmic pressure just shy of pushing her over the edge.

She needed something else, something—

He slid a finger inside her and she clamped around him, rolling her hips against him. Oh yeah, that was exactly what she needed.

Taking his cues from her body's response, he slid a second finger in and pushed deep inside her. Curling his fingers, he curved them up so they brushed against that oh-so sensitive spot she usually only found on her own. Instead of withdrawing and pushing back in her, he started stroking inside her right against that sensitive section of her body.

Her senses went into overload.

She slammed her hands against the couch, digging her fingers into the soft material so she wouldn't hurt his head as he continued his beautiful assault. The wicked way he continued caressing her combined with the constant pressure of his tongue was too much.

Without warning she surged into orgasm, her hips jolting off the couch and against his face as it slammed into her. Pleasure singed all her nerve endings from the onslaught. She arched back against the couch, loving the little growl of approval he made against her spread lips.

She wasn't sure how long the orgasm lasted but it seemed to go on forever until finally she fell back against the couch, breathing hard, feeling completely boneless and sated.

When he looked up at her, his expression was primal as he grabbed her hips and shifted her so that she fell back flat against the couch.

Moving like a predator, he covered her body with his, capturing her mouth in a hungry, dominating kiss that left her breathless. She moaned into him, tasting her release, something that was much more erotic than she'd ever imagined.

She reached between them and cupped his covered erection. Soon she was going to strip him down to nothing and give him just as much pleasure as he'd given her.

When he encircled her wrist, stopping her, she jerked back in surprise. "What?" she asked.

He lifted her arm above her head, pinning it against the couch. Just as quickly he did the same to the other, rendering her completely helpless. She loved feeling that way underneath him, knowing he could give her exactly the kind of pleasure she'd fantasized about.

"I told you what I was going to do to you," he murmured, a dark edge to his voice that made her nipples stand up, begging for attention.

Not trusting her voice, she nodded. He'd told her he was going to go down on her until she passed out from sheer exhaustion. But he couldn't have meant that, right?

He captured her mouth again, holding her arms in place as she writhed against him. Her hard nipples brushed against his shirt, the sensation wildly stimulating as she fantasized about what it would be like to have skin on skin contact.

When he shifted slightly so he could hold her wrists in place with one hand only to cup her mound and start teasing her with his other, she realized he'd been serious about his intentions.

At the thought, another orgasm almost tore from her.

The more time she spent with him, the more it hurt to realize he wasn't looking for anything serious. But he was so giving and sweet and the fact that he was solely focusing on her pleasure was kind of insane. She knew things between them would be over soon, and it hurt more than she wanted to admit, so she was going to enjoy every second of time with this man.

CHAPTER ELEVEN

"What?" Neal snarled, answering his burner phone on the first ring. He'd received a text from his contact a couple hours ago telling him that Taylor was on her way to the office. His contact had found that out from one of the security team members. So Neal had headed there, ready to follow her after she left. He knew where she lived but doubted she'd be returning to her home. Following her should have been easy enough.

But the incompetent moron he'd hired had fucked everything up by opening fire on Taylor and her security team. He said he'd just wanted to scare them. The company vehicles were all bullet resistant, something his contact knew but Neal hadn't ordered *him* to scare Taylor. He'd told the man he'd be taking care of that portion of his plan personally. Neal didn't want anyone going after her but him at this point and he thought he'd made himself perfectly clear.

Apparently not.

He needed to personally take her so he could get his damn money back, not scare her into fucking hiding.

Now thanks to massive stupidity, Neal was terrified he wouldn't be able to hunt her down and get his money. He'd have to go on the run if that happened. He didn't want to flee from the Russians but it would be his only option. Because he wasn't letting Alexei get his hands on him.

Though he wanted to shout at his contact for his stupidity, Neal took a deep breath and forced himself to hide his anger as he continued. "Were you able to track her or find out anything about where she's gone?"

There was a long pause. "No. The team has closed ranks. Anyone on this security detail has strict instructions not to talk to anyone about it, per Escobar's orders."

Damn it. "Does anyone suspect you're helping me?"

"No. I only know by chance. I called to talk to one of the guys, supposedly about something else, and asked what the deal was with her and Hugh and the whole situation. He clammed up and said if I had questions to talk to Escobar. He was all apologetic about it, but I'm getting nothing from anyone.

I can't be too eager asking either or they might suspect. And where's my fucking thank you for the risk I took tonight? I barely got away before the cops showed up."

Neal's jaw clenched once. The guy wanted a thank you? He wanted to lash out, but he couldn't. Not yet. He didn't respond fast enough because the man continued.

"And where's my money? I haven't been paid since before Vegas." His voice was heated, not that Neal cared.

So that's what the stupid shooting was about. Neal bet the man wanted more money for his 'help'. Moron. "I can meet at our regular place soon but it has to be before sunrise. I can't take the risk of being seen by anyone." They met at a park on the beach for all their cash drop-offs. It was public enough during the daytime, but at night it was perfect because it was empty of people. And there weren't any CCTVs anywhere in the direct vicinity. Ideal for what he planned to do next.

"I can be there in an hour. After this I'm done. I can't keep taking risks for you." His contact's voice had lost some of its heat.

"I understand. I'll be leaving town soon anyway." Which was true. Neal would be leaving town as soon as he killed this moron and got what he needed from Taylor. If anyone else got in the way he'd kill them too. He hoped it didn't come to that though because more dead bodies was a hassle.

As soon as they disconnected Neal grabbed a suppressor from his bag. He could attempt to kill the man with a knife, but a gun would be easier. The guy might be security personnel but he wasn't fucking bulletproof. He didn't think Neal had a reason to kill him so he wouldn't be ready for an attack. Even if the guy was wearing a Kevlar vest, Neal wasn't taking any chances. He'd shoot him right in the head.

He would just hide in the trees and kill him when he got close enough. The body would be found once the park opened, probably when an early morning jogger stumbled on him. Not that he cared now. He was going to be out of the country soon, leaving everything behind. After this, he'd get his money from Taylor then kill her. If he couldn't get the money, he was gone, dropping off the radar for good.

Alexei might be a scary bastard, but Neal was only one man. Surely they wouldn't spend years of resources on him. If he could just stay on the move for a while, never settling anywhere, maybe he could really outrun everyone.

CHAPTER TWELVE

Wearing a towel, Roman exited the bathroom to find the bed he'd shared with Taylor empty. He started to frown when the scent of coffee hit him. Waking up next to an incredibly sexy woman—who wore Wonder Woman panties, something he was still laughing about—and now coffee was already made, felt almost perfect. Especially since he didn't have to worry about his brother stealing his coffee.

Despite all the crap going on, being with Taylor was right where Roman wanted to be. He loved his job and his life, but right now he didn't want to be anywhere else but with her. The rightness of it, especially so soon after meeting her, floored him. What terrified him more; he couldn't see going back to his life without her in it. It would be like going from living in color to black and white. The thought was extreme but . . . she'd gotten under his skin. He shook that thought off and dressed. He didn't have time to analyze whatever was going on between them.

Minutes later he found Taylor lounging on the couch he'd made her climax on multiple times last night, her laptop in her lap and a purely evil grin on her face. She might deny it, but she did evil genius well. She had on jeans and a T-shirt with a storm trooper wearing earphones and DJing. He laughed out loud at the picture, causing her to look up.

Evil genius smile morphed into a sensual one as she looked him over from head to toe. Then she blushed adorably. "Morning," she murmured, her cheeks turning even redder.

Which was damn cute. She'd tried to go down on him last night, multiple times, but he'd needed everything to be about her. And . . . he wouldn't have been in control if he'd let her do what she wanted to him. Right now he felt as if he was walking a razor's edge and she had the ability to push him over it. Especially if she'd wrapped those pretty lips around his hard length. Even thinking about it and his dick woke up.

It was a primal thing, the only way he'd known how to take care of her in this fucked up situation. He couldn't even describe it to himself how much he'd liked bringing her so much pleasure.

Over and over.

From the pink in her cheeks, clearly she was remembering everything. Good. He wanted everything they'd done stamped into her memory bank.

"Morning. Sleep well?" he asked.

She snorted and slid her computer off her lap. "What do you think?" Blush gone, she stood and crossed the distance to him, wrapping her arms around his waist.

He pulled her into a tight hug, dropping a light kiss on her mouth, loving how open she was with affection. He resisted the urge to deepen it because he had a feeling they'd end up naked and on the floor if he did. "If you didn't then I clearly did something wrong. Which means I need to practice more." He dropped his voice as he said it, which earned him another blush.

She seemed to forget how to speak for a moment then slightly shook her head. "There's coffee in the kitchen and uh, I think I might have found something on Neal's whereabouts."

There was something in her tone that made him pause. As he headed for the kitchen, she followed and he could practically sense the nervousness rolling off her. "Well?"

She took a deep breath. "Hear me out before you say no."

Oh yeah, that didn't bode well for him. He nodded as he started to pour himself a mug. "Okay."

"I did a lot of digging into Neal's background this morning."

He frowned. "You haven't been up that long."

"Well . . . I woke up at three and worked for a couple hours. You looked so peaceful sleeping I didn't want to bother you."

Roman didn't respond, but he was beyond surprised he hadn't stirred.

"Anyway, I did a lot of digging earlier and when I woke up again not too long ago something was bothering me. There were a few emails referencing a sale of a boat, but nothing directly to him. To this corporation. I've never heard of the corporation though, not being linked directly to Powers Group. So I started digging into it and I can't be sure without more investigating, but I think it's a front for Neal. For what, I have no idea, but I don't think it's for anything real. Using the information on the 'business', I tracked down that boat. It's still owned by the company and according to credit card records from the same company, it's docked at a local marina."

"What kind of boat?"

"Forty-foot cruiser . . . The type someone could stay on. Live on, if need be." She bit her bottom lip, watching him expectantly.

Wow, she was good. *Really* good. "You think Lynch is on it?"

She shrugged. "Probably not, but it's worth checking out, right?"

"Yes, it is worth checking out. The police can do it immediately."

She bit her bottom lip even harder and shook her head. "How am I supposed to explain to them what I found?"

"Did you break any laws gaining the information?"

Taylor looked down and crossed her arms over her chest, but didn't answer.

"Damn it," he muttered.

Clearly exasperated, she threw up her hands. "What I did was only a little illegal. And if we see that he's there, we can call the police—anonymously. He might not even be there, but it's a lead and I don't want to pass it up. And I don't want to give the police bad intel and have them waste resources when we could just check."

He half-smiled, shaking his head. "Only a little illegal." Her eyes widened as she looked at him in semi-shock. "What?" he demanded.

"I've never seen you smile like that before. And that doesn't even really count, but . . . it looks good on you." She grinned, sidling closer and wrapping her arms around him. She wiggled slightly, playfully rubbing her breasts against him. It didn't matter that they were clothed, she definitely wasn't wearing a bra and he could feel her hard nipples protruding through her shirt. He bit back a groan.

Fuck. He was so screwed. He set his coffee cup down and grabbed her hips, holding her close. "Are you seriously trying to use your sex appeal to get me to do what you want?"

"Absolutely. And logic. *Mainly* logic. We need to check this out. It's the middle of the day, we can go just the two of us and not tell a soul. I trust Escobar but I don't want anyone to know about this. What if one of the security team members is involved and they tip off Neal? I can't risk that. Hugh deserves justice. The less people that know, the better. If we tell the cops and we're wrong, they waste a lot of resources and risk tipping him off anyway. A team of cops showing up? He's going to see that. But two people—"

"One person," he bit out. "If we do this, I'm the only one checking out the boat. You will at no time reveal yourself publicly anywhere. *Anywhere.* Got it?"

"So you're saying yes?" She practically jumped up and down with glee.

"I'm saying you'll leave the checking out to me," he muttered. He hated the idea, but she was right on all counts. If they could call in an anonymous tip on Lynch and get him arrested, the slimy bastard would flip on the guy who'd shot at Roman. Which would eliminate all threats to Taylor.

That was the carrot she was dangling in front of Roman and she had to know it. To finally get her safe, to get the men responsible for coming after her and killing her friend, was too much to pass up.

Roman knew he could keep her safe too. That wasn't an issue. And he agreed that the less people who knew what they were doing the better. Keeping the knowledge of this to just the two of them literally eliminated any potential leaks. He didn't like it, but he also didn't like sitting around doing nothing. He'd planned to get her out of here today and into a new place anyway. They could make a couple stops before hitting their new safe house. "You're going to need to change into less noticeable clothes. At least your shirt. Something plain. And we're going to have to make a couple stops before we head there."

She rolled up once on the balls of her feet, but it seemed as if she was restraining herself from jumping up and down.

"And," he stressed, "you do whatever I say, when I say it. If I say run, you start sprinting away. Nothing I say is up for debate."

"Even if you ask me to strip naked in public?"

His lips twitched. "Yep."

She nodded once. "Deal."

* * *

"What are you doing? Did you see him?" Taylor demanded the second Roman slid back into the SUV.

He got into the middle seat instead of the front seat since she was sitting there and he wanted to be close to her. The windows were darkly tinted and it was almost impossible to see inside. They'd been parked along the exterior of the marina for the last hour, not in the actual parking lot, but on the curb against the public sidewalk that lined the southeast side of it.

Oversized, white benches and clusters of big palm trees lined the walk, making it a perfect place for people to jog and walk their dogs. The sidewalks were triple the width of normal ones and this section was made specifically for that reason; so locals could exercise and stay active in their community.

Unfortunately it meant there were a lot of damn people around and he needed to get onto Lynch's boat unseen.

"No, but I don't think anyone's on the boat. All the blinds were open and I couldn't see anyone moving around inside. There were too many people around though. Some kind of open house type thing on the boat next door." He was pretty sure they were trying to sell the neighboring boat. Next time he was going to approach as a salesman of sorts. Just act confident and enter the boat. If Lynch was inside, he'd just disarm the fucker and call the cops. If he wasn't, Roman would play stupid and get the hell out of there, hopefully without being shot by the owner.

"So what are you doing back here?" She was practically jumping out of her seat as she squirmed there, wanting immediate results.

He shot her a look. "You do investigative work, Taylor. I need to wait before heading back over there."

She let out a frustrated sigh. "I know, I *know*. I'm just being impatient. I get that you can't just loiter around his boat without being suspicious."

"His?"

"I'm calling it that until I know otherwise. I have a good feeling about this." She reached up and fingered the blonde wig they'd gotten for her, the new weight of it probably bothering her.

It was likely unnecessary considering she wasn't getting out of the SUV, but he wanted her in disguise. She also had on a small white fedora-style hat with a blue ribbon around it. Combined with the blue and white striped shirt with three-quarter length sleeves—she'd informed him the shirt was something called a French sailor style. Whatever it was, she looked casual and the style was perfect for hanging around the marina. She looked like she was ready to head out for a day of sailing. So if anyone saw her—and they wouldn't since she wasn't leaving the damn vehicle—she'd blend in.

He slipped off his own ball cap and sunglasses as she asked, "So, how long are you going to wait to try again?"

Roman scrubbed a hand over his face. "Half an hour to an hour."

Sighing, she scooted closer to him, laying her head on his shoulder. "Thanks for doing this."

He didn't want her thanks. Shifting slightly, he tightened his arm around her shoulders, loving the feel of her up against him. She was a perfect fit. When she turned to look up at him, he was once again captured by her bright blue eyes. Every time he looked at her he was struck by how much he just plain liked this woman. No doubt the attraction was incendiary but what he felt for her was different than anything he'd experienced before.

"What's that look?" she asked.

"Nothing." Leaning down, he nipped her bottom lip between his teeth, unable to resist a quick taste.

When her cheeks flushed and she let out a moan, leaning into him, he pulled back, breathing hard from a simple kiss.

"We can't do anything," he murmured, unwilling to risk her safety.

"Tease," she muttered.

He snorted. "A tease? Last night there was follow-through."

When she just looked at him, that simmering hunger right beneath the surface, he glanced around, looking at his surroundings. He wanted to get inside her so badly his dick was already hard and aching. Nothing was out of the ordinary but . . . "Fuck, you're trying to kill me. We can't do anything here."

"Not even fool around a little?" she whispered, the atmosphere of the SUV subtly changing.

There was no way in hell because he knew he'd never stop at just kissing her. And the truth was, it would be beyond irresponsible. He glanced around again, his erection almost painful by now. He desperately wanted to take her here, right where they were close enough to people to see them but not be seen. The thought of it was hot. But it would be a huge security lapse, because the moment she touched his cock, there was no way in hell he'd be able to concentrate on anything but that. "I can't risk your safety like that," he finally said, turning back to her.

Her smile fell but she didn't seem angered, just disappointed. "You realize you're making me want you even more." She let out an overdramatic sigh. "And you're right but no more teasing. Last night was amazing but I want everything from you soon."

"Everything? Does that include..." He trailed off as he reached out for her. He slid his hand down her side, over her hip and around to her backside. He cupped her hard enough that she understood his intent. "Here too?" Normally he had a filter but apparently he'd lost it. Being with Taylor did that to him because he wanted to claim every inch of her. She wasn't like any other woman he'd been with. Everything about her was so open and honest.

Her eyes went wide, as if she'd never considered the possibility. Her pretty mouth opened once, then snapped shut. She stared at him for a long moment, clearly thinking. When she spoke next, her voice was raspy, uneven. "It's something we can discuss at a later date."

He grinned then, unable to help himself. "At least it's not off the table."

Just like that her gaze went heavy-lidded as it dropped to focus on his mouth. "I swear if you smile at me like that again, all bets are off and I'm jumping you."

Almost against his will, he did smile, full-on. Something he rarely did.

To his surprise she covered her face with her hands and shook her head. "You're a menace," she said, groaning.

For the first time in . . . hell if he could remember, Roman felt lighter, more at peace. The situation notwithstanding, being around Taylor was a breath of fresh air. He was insanely attracted to her, but he genuinely *liked* her. Way more than was good for his sanity.

After another forty-five minutes of waiting—and flirting—he changed shirts. She stared at him hungrily when he'd stripped, her clear lust setting him on fire and making him think of nothing but what it would be like once they were finally alone and able to act on their need. After he was dressed he put on a fedora-style hat himself, then headed out. But not before checking the small caliber weapon he'd left for Taylor. Because even if the threat level was low, he sure as hell wasn't leaving her unarmed. She knew a little about weapons thanks to her former boss, Hugh. He'd still watched her handle it and made sure she knew how to use it.

He returned from his scouting mission less than ten minutes later and found the weapon he'd given her on the backseat. The magazine was empty and loose bullets lay scattered on the floorboards. Roman's heart lurched as the bottom of his world fell out.

She'd been taken.

CHAPTER THIRTEEN

On the other side of the marina, Taylor folded her arms over her chest as she watched the man sitting on a white bench across from her. After basically kidnapping her—at gunpoint—he'd told her they were taking a stroll so they could chat.

He'd been incredibly polite about it, but that didn't matter. Maybe it even made it worse. The man had somehow opened the locks on the SUV she'd been in with a keyfob. He clearly had some sort of master electronic key. Which wasn't unheard of. But it was impressive—and scary. Terror streaked through her, the jagged edges piercing all her nerve endings as she tried to keep her cool. More than anything she was a little numb, which was the only thing keeping her from hyperventilating.

He'd grabbed the gun Roman had left for her and within seconds the man had taken it apart, emptying the bullets. Then he'd ordered her to come with him so they could chat for a few minutes. When a mother with a double stroller had paused by the SUV to tie her shoe he'd given Taylor a deadly, speculative look. As if to say he didn't care who got hurt if she didn't cooperate.

So Taylor had gone with him. But only because they were still in a public place, and she didn't want anyone else to get hurt. If he'd tried to get her into a vehicle she'd have screamed and fought for all she was worth. She'd rather get shot than be kidnapped. People walked by every few minutes and cars drove past on a consistent basis. None of that would help her if he decided to pump her full of bullets though. A shiver rolled down her spine as she imagined it happening.

"You and I are in a bit of a quandary," the man finally spoke, his slight accent betraying his heritage. She wasn't actually sure if he was Russian but that was what she'd dubbed him in her head. His dark aviator-style sunglasses with silver rims made it impossible to see his eyes. He was huge, with broad shoulders, but his build was more sleek than muscular.

She glanced around, wishing Roman would somehow find them. Her heart beat an erratic tattoo in her chest, thumping out of control so loudly blood rushed in her ears. She and the Russian hadn't gone far, but it was out of sight from the

SUV and the dock where Roman was. If he was back from his recon mission, he'd be looking for her. "I can't see how that's possible when I don't even know you." But she guessed that he must be working for Neal. That thought made a cold sliver of fear skitter over her skin. He could have just killed her in the SUV though, she reminded herself. Whoever this guy was wanted her alive. Because bringing her out of the SUV to kill her in a public place didn't make any sense.

"True, but we have a mutual acquaintance."

"So you're working for that bastard?" she asked, unable to hide the bite of anger from her voice. Because really, who else could he be working for? She might have suspected he was the man who'd come after her at Vadim's house, but this man had dark hair and tattoos. The description of the man Roman had interacted with was so plain and unassuming. Not this guy. This man was memorable, like a jungle animal roaming the streets wearing a black suit that did absolutely nothing to hide the fact that he was a predator. Which meant Neal had *two* guys working for him.

To her surprise, the man snorted. "*For* him? Lynch owes my boss money. And Lynch told me that you stole his money."

"I didn't steal anyone's money. And how did you know where I was today?" Because she and Roman had been incredibly careful coming here.

He paused for a long moment, watching her, though all she could see was her own reflection in the sunglasses. Which was pretty unnerving, and was probably why he wore the damn things. That and the way he was so still was freaking her the hell out.

"I saw your friend scouting Lynch's boat. Then I spotted you messing with your hair when he got into your SUV. I wasn't even certain it was you because of the wig, but you have a beautiful face. Hard to forget. This," he glanced around them, "was just an opportunity I couldn't pass up. Now tell me what we're going to do about Lynch's money—my money."

A surge of adrenaline pumped through her at the confirmation that she'd been right in tracking down Neal's boat. That meant he could be nearby, close enough to bring down even. Was he on the boat? Maybe Roman had already called the cops. She hoped so. Unfortunately she was pretty sure this guy was a hit man of sorts. If he collected money for someone maybe he was more of an enforcer. Which was terrifying.

She cleared her throat, trying to tamp down her nerves. "Neal Lynch stole from the company I work for. That money has been returned to Powers Group." She decided not to confirm that yes, she was the one who'd liberated the funds from that thieving monster. "So whatever he owes you is on him. If he owes you so much, why not just take his boat?"

The Russian stilled, his head cocking ever so slightly to the side. "I have checked. The boat is not his property."

She shook her head. "The boat belongs to one of his fake corporations. It's his and it's worth over five hundred thousand." And as far as she'd been able to find out, he hadn't bought it with Powers Group money.

"My boss only takes clean products."

She frowned, not understanding. "The boat is clean. I mean, it's under a corporation's name, but he could transfer it to you. Hell, *I* could transfer it to you or whoever you work for with a clean bill of sale. Title and everything. The owner would be responsible for future docking fees wherever they keep it and yearly tax fees, but . . . it's clean."

Another long pause. "Right now Lynch is being protected. It is in my interests that he is not arrested. Yet. If you transfer his property to me, he is fair game. If not . . . things could get messy. Starting with that friend of yours."

Taylor's hands balled into fists, her jaw tightening. Threatening the man she cared about, especially after she'd just lost someone, wasn't in this guy's best interests. All her instincts told her to lash out, but she reined in the stupid part of her brain and took a deep breath. "Just so we're clear. If I transfer ownership of the boat, Neal is no longer protected? And you will leave me and my friends alone?"

"Correct."

"Fine." She had no idea who this man was, though she could guess considering some of the tattoos on his fingers. She'd done enough reading that she recognized some of them. And she knew there was a Russian mob presence here and in surrounding areas. Combined with his accent and the mention of his boss—she didn't even want to know the name of the man he was working for.

The man reached into his jacket pocket and for one moment she tensed, thinking he was going for the gun he'd holstered earlier. Instead he pulled out her cell phone, then battery. He handed both pieces to her. "I'll call this phone with details soon."

Nodding, and trying not to show how much she was trembling, she stood and slipped the battery back into her phone. Turning it on, she clasped it close to her chest, her fingers wrapping around it like a lifeline. It didn't hide the subtle tremor racking her body. "You better freaking *call.*" Not come after her with a gun. Though she didn't say it out loud it was pretty clear she was implying it.

He simply nodded and she took a few steps away from him, back in the direction of where he'd taken her from. He didn't move from his spot.

Heart racing and sweat dotting her upper lip and forehead, she turned away from him and started walking, her legs shaking. Swiping her code into her phone, she tapped on the camera icon. Then she turned around again, still moving away from him. The man was standing, his body turned toward hers, but he wasn't making any threatening gestures.

She was careful about it, but she took his picture as she held her cell phone against her chest, knowing she needed this to figure out who he was. His jaw tensed, as if he knew what she'd done.

She turned and ran, her lungs burning as she sprinted down the sidewalk. Avoiding a couple joggers, she jumped to the left and risked a glance behind her as she fled. He was walking in the other direction, not coming after her. Elation surged through her but she didn't stop her getaway.

Slowing to a fast walk instead of a sprint that would draw more attention, she rounded the corner onto the sidewalk that ran along the southeast side of the marina.

Less than thirty seconds later she spotted the SUV. Her heart pounded erratically in her chest, the staccato thump insistent, blood rushing in her ears. Maybe Roman wasn't even back yet—He appeared from around the other side of the vehicle, his expression tense and his cell phone held up to his ear.

He barked something into it and dropped his arm as he rushed toward her onto the sidewalk. She threw herself at him, wrapping her arms around his neck. "We need to leave. Now!" Winded from fear and running, she sucked in deep breaths.

It was clear he wanted to argue as he scanned behind her, looking for any threats but he nodded and ushered her to the passenger side of the SUV. After shutting her door he rounded the vehicle and hurried to the driver's side and slammed the door.

"You hurt?" he demanded, his voice shaking with what she recognized as worry as he started the engine.

"No, but we have a problem. And a solution I think." As he drove, she launched into what had happened, leaving nothing out.

"You *what?*" he roared, when she got to the part where she'd taken the man's picture.

She cringed at the censure in his voice, but didn't apologize. "We need to know who he is. And on the bright side we at least have confirmation that Neal owns that boat."

Roman was silent, his jaw clenching in clear anger as he carefully maneuvered through traffic. She had no idea where they were going and didn't think she should ask. When he pulled into the parking lot of a local burger place, she broke her silence. "What's going on?"

Instead of answering, he pulled out his cell phone and glanced at his screen. He typed in a text and after a response pinged back he focused on her, his expression fierce, intense.

And incredibly sexy. Something she was surprised she noticed for the jagged nerves still thrumming through her. "Roman—"

He moved so fast she didn't see him coming, his mouth covering hers with a surprising gentleness. His lips were insistent against hers, his tongue teasing the seam of her lips as he demanded entrance. But there was still a softness to his kiss as he cupped her face with both hands, holding her in place. As if she was precious to him.

Unable to stop the moan that escaped, she leaned into him, grabbing on to his shoulders as her tongue danced against his. The adrenaline that had spiked inside her earlier surged again at the sound of a knock on Roman's window. She jumped back, breathing hard, while he didn't seem fazed as he turned toward a waiting Escobar.

Where had he come from? Roman must have let him know they'd be here. Some of her panic subsided, but she was still shaky from everything that had happened.

Escobar gave her a hard look as Roman got out of the vehicle. Oh yeah, he was probably mad she and Roman had left without telling the security team earlier. She should probably feel bad about that, but didn't. Even with the scary Russian man temporarily detaining her at gunpoint, they'd found out some valuable information. Now that they knew where Neal was, or would be staying, they had an advantage.

Taylor got out and hurried around to the other side. Roman was quietly filling in Escobar on what she'd told him the Russian wanted her to do. And she also heard Escobar telling Roman that the police had found Neal's clothes and murder weapon from the day of the shooting stashed above some ceiling tiles in an empty conference room. As she walked around the vehicle she saw a waiting SUV that looked like one of the Powers Group's and a blue minivan next to it with one of their security guys sitting in the passenger seat. He gave her a half-wave.

As she reached Roman and Escobar she started to ask them what was going on when Escobar held out his hand. "I need your phone."

"Why?"

"He's giving you a new one that can't be tracked. All your calls will be forwarded to the new phone. And he needs the picture you took," Roman said, his voice all business, as if they hadn't just shared a heated kiss.

She handed her phone over and Escobar handed her another one, a slightly newer version of her current cell. "Thanks."

Escobar nodded but kept his focus on Roman. "We're ready now."

Roman slung an arm around her shoulders and led her to the waiting minivan. He slid into the backseat with her and as they drove away, she saw a security guy from the other SUV get out and head for the one she and Roman had just vacated. "Okay, what's going on?" she finally demanded.

"We're moving to a secure location now. Escobar and Garza are coming with us. They're the only two completely vetted by Christiansen's security check."

"Wait, *what?*"

"Wyatt did a check on all of Powers Group security employees and most are cleared but Escobar and Garza are the only ones he says he trusts completely to come with us. And I agree with him."

Escobar just grunted from the front as he looked at her cell phone.

Roman continued. "We're heading to another safe house with only the four of us in this vehicle privy to its location."

She decided not to point out that she actually didn't know its location yet.

"Wyatt's sending in a small team, including my brother, to stay with us for the next few days. They'll be here in a couple hours."

"He can't want to hire me that badly." Because what Mr. Christiansen was doing seemed excessively generous.

"You found Neal Lynch before the police. Or at least his boat. You're clearly good at what you do so don't be surprised by how badly he wants to hire you. But . . . this has more to do with Vadim. He and Angel are on their way back from their—"

"No!" Oh God, she felt terrible if he'd come back early from his honeymoon.

Roman's expression softened and he shook his head. "It's not because of you. Not entirely. I talked to Angel and it sounds as if they were both going stir crazy on an island. They were ready to get back home."

"Wait, when did you talk to her? And when did you set any of this up? I wasn't gone for that long."

To her surprise, he scrubbed a hand over his head and looked almost sheepish. "I've been setting this up since yesterday but I made most of the calls and set everything into motion when I was scouting Lynch's boat."

She'd known he planned to move them to a new safe house but an outside security team was a big deal. "You're not..." She shot a glance to the front seat and lowered her voice as she looked back at Roman, even though she was pretty sure the two men in the front could still hear her. "You're not paying for this security detail are you? This all sounds really expensive."

He blinked, as if she'd really surprised him. "No, but I would. You're worth it." He said it so matter-of-fact, he left her speechless as he continued. "Right now the only thing that matters is keeping you safe."

"Got some news. Good and bad," Escobar said from the front. He held up her phone, which had now been switched off. "I recognize the man from the picture and it's bad. Did a quick check to make sure but it's Alexei Lagunov. Enforcer for the Russian mob. Deadly reputation, which I believe is earned."

The blood in her veins turned icy, chilling her from the inside out. She'd had an idea the guy was bad news but hearing it confirmed was terrifying. As a shudder snaked through her, Roman took her hand in his. Her hand was clammy but she didn't care. His touch grounded her.

"Can you really do what you told him? Transfer the boat to his boss?" Escobar asked.

She nodded.

A long moment passed in which Roman and Escobar seemed to have a silent conversation. "What?" she asked either Roman or Escobar. She didn't care who answered.

She wasn't sure if Garza knew what was going on and wasn't planning on spelling it out. She'd worked with the other man and liked him well enough. He was really quiet, but very skilled according to Hugh. Her boss had used him often for his personal security, which made her feel better about him being here.

"I think it's in your best interest to do it. The Russian mob . . . they're not forgiving. While you have nothing to do with Lynch or the money he owes, you're now on their radar and that's a bad place to be, especially when you've made them a promise. Give them what they want. When they're out of the picture and Lynch is fair game, we call the police. Which we could do now. If that happens, I don't know if they'll take it out on you. They want their money, bottom line. The choice is up to you though."

She swallowed hard and looked at Roman, a small part of her wondering if he'd judge her for what she was going to do. It wasn't even a decision really. "I'm doing it." Because she wasn't stupid enough to piss off the Russian mob.

Roman let out a relieved breath. "Good. If you didn't I was going to ask Vadim to."

"You said something about good news?" she asked, looking at Escobar while still holding Roman's hand.

"Yeah." His expression was grim though, not exactly lining up with the concept of 'good news'. "Clayton Gibson, one of my guys, was found dead earlier this morning at a park. Shot six times in the face and chest. He had a vest on, which is odd enough, and . . . Anyway, I did some checking into his financials—deep checking—and it looks like he was Lynch's partner. He'd been taking extra payoffs from Lynch, through the company, but to an offshore account. It was in his sister's name, which is why we missed it the first time, but once I started looking harder it wasn't difficult to figure out what he's been up to. There's more evidence against him, including some credit card receipts from Vegas during the time frame you were there. I've already emailed you and the police everything we've found, but I'm pretty sure he was Lynch's partner."

She leaned back against the seat, stunned, and a little numb. She hadn't known Gibson well but they'd traveled together before for work. He'd been on Neal's security detail many times and whenever she'd traveled with him or Hugh she'd chatted with the guy. He'd seemed normal enough. She should feel relieved that one of her problems was gone but she felt . . . ugh. She just felt depressed.

Sighing, she leaned her head on Roman's shoulder. "As soon as we hear from the Russian enforcer," which felt weird saying out loud, "and I take care of everything, then what?"

"Then we call the cops on Lynch," Roman said.

"What if—"

Escobar shook his head, cutting her off as if he knew what she was going to ask. "The guys you saw back at the parking lot, they're going to be watching the marina too. Just because the Russians are watching doesn't mean we can't too. Once we get a bead on Neal, that fucker isn't going anywhere."

"You don't think we should just call the police on him?" *She* didn't, but she really needed to hear them say it too. If they called the cops and Neal was arrested and the Russian mob didn't get their money—yeah, she wasn't taking a chance they took it out on her for losing their money.

Roman and Escobar both snorted at the same time, the unified reaction making her smile even in the middle of the most craptastic situation she could have imagined.

CHAPTER FOURTEEN

Roman knocked on the door of the bathroom Taylor was in. The luxury condo Wyatt had put them in was huge, with four rooms and the place spanning the entire floor. More importantly, it was secure. Apparently Wyatt owned it so he was putting it to good use.

"Come in," Taylor called out. She looked up when he stepped inside and caught his gaze in the mirror. She'd pulled her shirt up and was attempting to put on another bandage by herself. He hated that she'd been hurt but she never mentioned it or acted injured so he'd almost forgotten about it. For a civilian, she'd been handling things so damn well it impressed him.

"I'll do that." Shutting the door behind him, he crossed the distance to her.

She turned to face him, her lips pulling up at the corners. "I can do it."

"I know, but it gives me an excuse to touch you," he murmured.

She made a pleased sound, but didn't respond as he started cleaning the small wound. He still couldn't believe how lucky she'd gotten. That being a relative term considering she'd been shot in the first place. At that thought he had more fantasies of strangling Neal Lynch.

"Can you lift your shirt higher?" he asked as he grabbed one of the white gauzy pads from the first aid kit. It had pretty much scabbed over but it was better to keep it covered while it was healing.

Wordlessly she pulled her shirt up and over her head. His fingers froze on the pad for a moment as his eyes fell to her bra and the gorgeous breasts it encased. The scraps of lace didn't do much to hide anything. Last night he'd seen every inch of her, had finally been able to savor sucking on those light brown nipples and full breasts while listening to her moan. He wasn't going to bother asking her what she was doing because it was pretty damn obvious.

And he was done with showing restraint. He shifted uncomfortably, his erection pushing insistently against his pants. "Escobar went to grab food and Garza is standing guard outside the condo. We've got about an hour until Wyatt's team gets here," he said, his voice surprisingly even for the lust surging through him. Moving quickly he secured the pad with the white adhesive roll from the kit.

Her responding grin was like a punch to his solar plexus. "What can we do in an hour?" Her voice was barely above a whisper.

The rational part of his brain told him to move slowly, to give her foreplay but after last night, after having a taste of her, of hearing how she sounded when she climaxed… Foreplay could come later. He needed to be inside her, feel her close around him. Reaching for the button of her dark jeans, he said, "Tell me if I hurt you."

She grabbed the hem of his shirt and tore it over his head, her movements almost frantic, mirroring the way he felt. Moments later they were both naked and before he could stop her—not that he wanted to—she was on her knees in front of him, her fingers wrapped around his erection.

The smile on her face as she looked at his cock and licked her lips was one of the hottest things he'd ever seen. When she leaned forward and wrapped that sexy mouth around his hard length, he groaned, letting his head fall back. But just for a second because he wanted to watch. He grasped the edge of the counter, his knuckles turning white.

Through heavy-lidded eyes he stared down at her, mesmerized as she sucked him deep in her mouth, making appreciative sounds as she stroked. When she shifted slightly, leaning forward to take him deeper, her hair fell from her shoulders. He dragged his fingers through her hair, loosely holding the back of her head as she moved.

His lower spine tingled as pleasure pulsed through him in waves. God, her *mouth*. Just the feel of her teasing him like this was almost too much. But watching his cock disappear in and out of her mouth—She gently cupped his balls and he knew he wouldn't last long. Fucking embarrassing, but damn, being naked with Taylor took away all his typical control.

He needed to get it back. To get her off before he came. Though it was almost painful to stop her, he rolled his hips back, pulling away from her.

She made a protesting sound, but when he reached under her arms and lifted her up, the heat in her bright eyes nearly undid him.

Unable to find his voice he reached between their bodies, cupping her mound. He felt her slickness even before he'd pushed a finger inside her. She coated him, the proof of her desire flooring him. She was this turned on for him, after going down on him.

Her fingers dug into his chest as she arched into his hold. He wanted nothing more than to capture her mouth with his and plunge his cock deep inside her. But he knew if he started kissing her he'd take her right here and now on the floor or counter. Which he planned to do, but he needed to get back some control first.

"Turn toward the mirror," he ordered.

She paused for a second but did as he said. Grabbing a condom from his pants, he ripped it open and quickly rolled it on as he turned to face her.

Her hands were on the counter and her legs spread as she watched him in the mirror. Moving behind her, he grabbed one of her hips and reached around to her front as he pulled her flush against his chest. Sliding his hand up her flat stomach he stopped under one of her breasts before cupping it.

He kept his gaze on her face, watching as she tracked his movements. Her breathing hitched up a notch when he flicked his thumb over her already hard nipple. Oh yeah, it wasn't going to take long to push her over the edge. Or him.

God, his entire body pulled tight with need, desire. He could hardly stand it, he wanted inside her so bad. Brushing her long hair forward, he leaned down and started feathering kisses along the back of her neck. "Touch your clit," he murmured.

She jerked against him, her butt rubbing against his erection at his order. He could do it, but he wanted to see her touch herself, to know that she had no problem when he gave orders in bed. Or against a bathroom counter.

He liked control in the bedroom, always had, and he knew he needed a partner who meshed with him on this level. He wasn't into chains and shit, but he did like to take control.

Without pause she reached between her legs and started stroking herself, her blue eyes locked on his in the mirror as he nipped down on one of her shoulders.

"Feel good?"

She nodded, her lips parted a fraction, eyes glazed with pleasure.

"Want to feel my cock in you?"

In response, she moaned, pushing back and wriggling against him. He couldn't help himself even if he'd wanted to. Grinning, he lightly pressed his teeth into her shoulder, raking over her skin.

He was so damn hard and she was so incredibly wet that when he nudged her entrance, he slid right in. She was tight, like he'd known she would be after feeling his fingers inside her, and he didn't want to be anywhere else but inside her tight, wet body.

Groaning, she arched back, pushing against him so that he slid fully to the hilt. She clutched onto the counter as her head fell forward, as if she was savoring the feel of him buried inside her.

Without moving, he slowly kissed and nipped his way across her back to her other shoulder, the feel of her soft skin perfection. "I didn't say you could stop touching yourself." There was an edge to his voice he knew she couldn't miss.

Her eyes snapped open, meeting his gaze in the mirror. For a moment he worried the way he was ordering her would make her pull back. Instead, her full lips curved into a wicked grin as she reached between her legs again and started stroking herself.

And wasn't that the hottest thing he'd ever seen.

Rolling his hips back, he pulled out before plunging deep inside her. Knowing how sensitive she was after last night, he cupped both her breasts and began teasing her nipples, gently at first. When he rolled and slightly pinched them, she jerked back against him, trying to make him increase his rhythm.

So he buried himself completely inside her and held onto one of her hips, keeping her tight against him. The pleasure that shot through him at the feel of her tight body had all his muscles tensing in anticipation. It wouldn't be long now. God, he needed her to come first. Craved the sounds she made.

Her eyes were dilated, her breathing uneven as she looked at him in the mirror. Sliding the hand down that had been holding her hip, he pushed hers out of the way and started stroking her clit in the rhythm he'd learned she needed.

Just like that, her inner walls spasmed and clenched around him as her orgasm slammed into her.

"Roman," she rasped out his name, a ragged moan on her lips.

He continued stroking her clit as her head fell forward, her eyes closing. She murmured his name and other indecipherable words as she came. He drank in the sight of her losing herself to her climax and let go of his control.

Unable to stop the groan that tore from him, he thrust into her over and over, his own release following on the heels of hers with a sharpness he hadn't expected. His balls pulled up tight and all the muscles in his body pulled taut as he let go.

"Taylor," he moaned, burying her face against her neck as he came down from his high. Wrapping his arm around her middle, he kept her close to his body, loving the feel of her back against his chest.

As their breathing returned to normal, he met her gaze in the mirror. Her eyes were bright and her cheeks flushed as she gave him an intimate smile.

"Remember what I said about not wanting anything serious?" he asked quietly.

She tensed in his hold and he could feel her inner walls clench around his now half-hard length. She nodded, her expression wary.

"I'm full of shit. We're going to be doing this again. A lot. And I'm not sharing you with anyone else." Because if they weren't serious she'd be free to date other people. The thought of that made something jealous and foreign flare inside him. Yeah, he didn't like that idea at all.

She grinned and wiggled against him, making him groan against her neck again. "Good, because I'm not sharing you either."

Fine by him.

Hating to do it, he pulled out of her and disposed of the condom as she turned to face him. "So . . .

you want to see where this thing between us goes?" he asked.

Nodding, she bit her bottom lip. "Yes. It's probably crazy to even entertain something between us right now, but . . . I feel like I'd really regret it if we didn't give whatever's happening between us a chance. Are we crazy?"

He let out a sigh of relief he hadn't realized he'd been holding. "Who cares if we are?" he murmured, brushing his lips against hers. God, he could lose himself in her all day. As he deepened the kiss, a sharp knock on the door made him pull back.

He'd heard the alarm briefly beep before it was turned off and had assumed it was Escobar returning since no one else knew the code. Still, moving on instinct, he pushed her behind him.

"Roman?" Escobar called out before he could say anything.

"Yeah."

"Taylor's getting a call. Unknown number."

They both sprang into action, hurriedly tugging their clothes on. Taylor was faster than him by a second, grabbing the door as Roman finished pulling his shirt over his head.

Escobar stood there, phone in hand. The ring was a soft chiming sound. She snagged it from the other man, but Roman plucked it from her before she could answer. She made a yelping sound, but he ignored her, stepping into the bedroom as he answered.

"Hello?"

There was a short pause. "Is Taylor available?" The slightly accented male voice gave away who the caller was. Or who Roman guessed it was.

"Alexei?"

Another pause, this time longer. "Who is this?"

"The friend of hers you threatened. She's going to help you get what you want, but then you have no reason to contact her again. And anything you say to her, goes through me. Understand?"

"I will speak only to her."

Roman snorted. "Then you're done. Good luck getting that five hundred thou for your boss." He hung up.

"Roman! Why did you do that?" Taylor sounded horrified, her expression matching her tone when he turned to look at her and Escobar.

Escobar answered before he could. "Because he had to establish ground rules. Someone like this only respects power and we need to let him know who's in control."

Exactly, Roman thought.

Taylor started to say something but the phone rang again. Unknown number. Roman answered. "Yes?"

"I will need confirmation from the woman that she will do what we request." There was an underlying note of impatience in his voice. And the terms were clearly vague in case this was being recorded.

"I'm putting you on speaker," Roman said, pressing the button. "She can hear you."

"How long will it take to transfer everything?" Alexei asked, his words clipped.

She looked at Roman as she spoke, her expression tense. "Not long. Couple hours at the most. I'll need someone to transfer everything to though."

For the next couple minutes Taylor talked to the Russian mob enforcer, writing down benign enough information for who the boat's title would be transferred to and she gathered what she'd need to make it happen. Roman figured she'd do that magic of hers, probably some of it illegal, and he was just counting down the seconds until this was all behind her. Behind them.

As soon as Taylor was done, Roman took the phone off speaker. "You still there?"

"Yes." A terse answer.

Roman nodded at Escobar, silently asking him to keep Taylor in the room as he left. Thankfully she didn't argue or try to follow as he strode from the room. He didn't give a shit that this guy was part of the mob. Roman had better training than most people on the planet and he'd been trained to kill in too many methods to count.

He wanted to make it clear to this man that if he tried to cross Taylor or come after her in any way, that he would be a dead man walking. The mob couldn't protect him from Roman if one hair on her head was touched. No force on earth could.

CHAPTER FIFTEEN

Panic detonated inside Neal as he hurried down the dock toward his boat and saw Alexei standing next to the vessel, his hands shoved in his pants' pockets. The sun had just set and the marina was quiet, with most people who lived here on their way to dinner at one of the nearby seafood restaurants. He'd been running errands all day, gathering all the money and IDs he'd stashed around the city in various places. It had been tedious and slow because he'd had to be extra careful about the places he retrieved his money from. He'd had to make sure he wasn't being followed or that the places he'd been to weren't under surveillance. All this was necessary in case he needed to go on the run. Which seemed to be a certain thing if he didn't find Taylor by the end of tomorrow.

His deadline.

So why the hell was Alexei here now? That familiar fear at seeing the big Russian slid through Neal's veins. As he neared the boat, he saw another man exiting the interior cabin, one of Neal's gym bags in his hand.

"What's going on?" he asked, trying to keep his voice civil. Alexei wasn't the kind of man you lost your temper with.

Alexei barely glanced at him as he surveyed the area. As if Neal wasn't worth his time. "My boss has decided to claim your boat as payment. You no longer owe him. My men are removing your belongings," he said, as the other man dropped the gym bag onto the dock close to Neal's feet.

"I have until tomorrow!" God, he needed a bump. Something to take the edge off. His fingers trembled and he went to grab at Alexei's arm, to beg if need be, but stopped himself at the last minute. He wasn't suicidal. His boat was supposed to have been his way out of here, a backup if he needed more money, a way to bribe officials if he crossed the border. Because this vessel was worth a lot.

Alexei acted as if Neal hadn't spoken. He pulled out his cell phone and started texting—texting!—as if he wasn't even there. A predator-like grin spread across Alexei's face as he sent his message.

Another surge of dread filled him as two more bags were dropped onto the dock. No, no, no. He needed the money this boat could give him. It was clean and matched one of his IDs. Fleeing the authorities in it would be easy. Now he had nothing but cash. And the money wouldn't last him long. "Alexei, please, I have until tomorrow. This boat is still *mine*. If your boss takes it he runs the risk of using stolen property."

Now those eerie, green eyes focused on Neal. "You plan on calling the police?"

Neal didn't miss the mocking note in his voice. He swallowed hard. "I'll report it stolen." He sounded braver than he felt and the words were bullshit. Something Alexei had to know.

The other man smiled then, once again reminding him of a shark. Involuntarily Neal took a small step back then inwardly cursed his weakness. When he reached into his jacket pocket Neal froze, certain the Russian was pulling out a gun. Instead he pulled out a sheaf of papers. He unfolded them and held them up. "Thank you for the very legal bill of sale."

No! Ice filled his veins, threading through him, leaving him frozen where he stood.

Alexei laughed, the first time Neal had ever heard the sound from the man. The sound was even more frightening than his smile. Continuing, the Russian shook his head. "I wish you could see your expression. You are a man with no honor and deserve everything you will get. What kind of man kills his own partner? You think I'm a monster, I know this. But I am loyal to my people. You . . . you are worthless."

Neal opened his mouth to respond, but no words would come out. His throat was dry, scratchy and—that was sirens in the distance. His head whipped around in their direction, not that it did any good. He couldn't actually see the police cars. Were they coming for him?

He looked back at Alexei and the smug, triumphant smile on the man's face was all he needed to confirm the truth. "You called the police?"

The Russian shook his head. "No. You angered a lot of people Mr. Lynch. My boss gets his payment and now the people who helped us get what they want. You in prison. Simple as that. Like I said before, you might want to just kill yourself. I don't think a man like you will do well in prison." He chuckled again then turned away from him, completely dismissing him.

Oh God. He had to move fast. To flee.

The sirens were getting louder. Closer.

Bending, he grabbed the bag with his extra cash. He looked inside to make sure it was still there.

Cash and burner phones. He could replace everything else.

Hefting the bag up, he started running. He had to get away from the marina.

Behind him he could hear the men laughing at him. Fuck them. He would escape. No matter what it took, he'd get away. The Russian's words rolled around in his head; 'the people who helped us'. What the hell? Only one person that he knew of wanted him in prison. Taylor Arenas.

Well, most of the employees at the Powers Group wanted him imprisoned or dead. Everyone had loved Hugh. But Taylor and maybe a few people from the IT department were the only ones smart enough to transfer his boat to the Russians.

He'd made sure that purchase was buried deep, under layers and layers so there would be no tracing it back to him. But that bitch must have figured it out.

It had to be her.

Even if it wasn't he didn't care. He was going to make her pay for everything she'd done. This whole situation was her fault. She'd told Hugh what he'd been up to. If she'd just kept her nose out of his business none of this would have happened. Hugh would still be alive and the company would be out a little cash.

No big deal.

But she'd thought she could just check up on him, like he was some common criminal. As he raced along the dock a plan formed in his mind. There was one more person he could turn to for help.

It was risky and would cost him every last cent he had to get what he needed to bring her down. But it would be worth it because if he did it right, she'd be dead and he'd be able to escape for the rest of his life without looking over his shoulder. He'd have to start over financially but it would be worth it with that bitch dead.

CHAPTER SIXTEEN

Three days later

Roman opened the back of the armored SUV door for Taylor and as she slid in, another wave of tears welled up. She swiped at them, willing them to stop. But it was useless.

Hugh's funeral had left her emotionally spent. Everyone from work—sans Neal—had been there. Not to mention hundreds of other people. Hugh had made a lot of contacts and friends over the years. A fair businessman who gave back to the community, he would definitely be missed by many. Especially by her. *So much.* She'd never forget the first big business deal she'd helped him with. He'd taken her and the others on the team out for a big celebration dinner, making her feel like she belonged somewhere and was doing something good for the first time in a long time. He'd made her feel like more than an employee, like she mattered. And he'd done the same thing for so many people because he'd truly cared.

"He'd have loved how many people showed up today," Taylor murmured, leaning her head on Roman. He'd been with her the past couple days, a steady rock. For once in her life she had no problem depending on someone for emotional support. Because right now, she needed it. Saying goodbye had been harder than she'd thought. She'd made a silent vow to him that she would see Neal brought down for what he'd done. That was the only thing that helped make her feel better.

Roman's arm tightened around her shoulders as Escobar started the engine. The last three days they'd basically been holed up in Wyatt Christiansen's condo. Despite what Escobar had said about her taking time off, she'd been working on different company projects, tying up anything she could this week just to keep busy and because she didn't want things to fall apart because Hugh was gone. Since she could work anywhere as long as she had her laptop it hadn't been an issue.

She knew she needed to ask Roman how much longer he'd be staying and what would happen between them from here, but she'd been feeling way too raw to say it in case he didn't give her the answer she wanted. She'd just needed to get through today. Now that the funeral was over, she knew it was time for the conversation. Because as much as she wanted him to, she knew he couldn't stick around and guard her until Neal was found.

She was still pissed he'd managed to get away. Neither the police nor the security team—all of whom Escobar had since fired for losing sight of him—had been able to track him down after he'd fled the marina. Alexei had actually called to apologize for not locking Neal down at the marina. The Russian had said he thought the cops would easily apprehend him and if she hadn't known better she might have believed the man truly felt bad.

"Yeah, Hugh would have," Escobar murmured from the front. He cleared his throat, almost nervously as he glanced at her in the rearview mirror. "Are you going to stay with the company now that he's gone?" he asked, the blunt question not exactly a surprise. He'd dropped hints the past couple days, clearly curious what her plan was.

It was subtle, but she felt Roman tense next to her. She wished she had an answer. "I don't know." Her voice sounded raspy and tired. The thought of going back to work for Powers Group without Hugh there was beyond depressing. "You?"

To her surprise, he shook his head. "I don't know either. The new CEO…" He shrugged, his face twisting into a momentary state of disgust before returning to its normal impassiveness.

The new guy was okay but the truth was, he wasn't Hugh. No one could replace him, not in the sense that mattered for Taylor. Because she'd been more loyal to the man than the company.

They drove in silence back to the condo, but the whole time stress built inside her. She hated being in this weird suspended state where she couldn't return to her apartment and needed guards in case Neal made a move against her.

It was like the man had basically disappeared off the grid. Even Vadim, who'd since returned to Vegas, was implementing all of his magic and running Neal's face through all his facial recognition software programs and he was coming up empty too.

When Escobar's phone rang, the soft chime seemed overly loud in the interior of the SUV, and she nearly jumped.

"Yeah," he answered, his tone clipped. "Hold on. I'm putting you on speaker." Without seeming to wait for a response, he connected to the vehicle's blue tooth system. "We can all hear you."

Taylor and Roman both straightened when Detective Durnin's brusque voice came over the line.

"Got good news for you guys. Taylor, you sitting down?"

"Yes." The only good news she could imagine right now was Neal being caught and prosecuted for his crimes. Her heart beat an out of control thump in her chest as she waited for him to speak again.

"Found Lynch's body late last night. Would have called sooner but I knew you'd be at the funeral." His voice softened the slightest bit.

"Body?" Roman asked, voicing what Taylor was thinking.

"Yeah and it's not pretty. From our investigation we know he owed some serious debts to the Russian mob. Off the record, I think he couldn't pay so they killed him."

Taylor shot Roman a glance but didn't say anything. They'd never told the police about their involvement in making sure the Russians got the money they were owed.

"Why do you think it's the Russians?" Roman asked.

There was a long pause, probably because the man was debating whether he should tell them or not. It was an ongoing investigation and while Taylor knew they couldn't be suspects because they'd been on virtual lockdown the last three days—and could all prove their whereabouts for pretty much every second of the last few days—he probably shouldn't tell them. When he spoke again, however, she guessed he felt bad about how everything had gone down.

"Hands, feet and another . . . important body part were missing. Even the face was too fuc—uh, messed up to positively identify. The only way we know it's him is because of his dental records. He had multiple fake IDs on him too, like he might have been planning to leave the country."

Taylor's stomach twisted at the thought of the torture he must have endured. And a dark part of her she hadn't realized existed inside her, was glad he'd suffered.

Roman's expression was grim. "You're sure it's him?"

"We're still going to check his DNA because of the high profile nature of the case, but . . . yeah. Barring anything unforeseen, I think we've got him."

Escobar, Roman and the detective talked for a couple more minutes but Taylor basically tuned it out. Relief and sadness warred inside her, both winning. Neal Lynch was dead and no longer a problem. And from the sound of it, he'd gotten what he deserved. But Hugh was still gone too and that just killed her.

"You can finally go home," Roman murmured as Escobar ended the call. He kissed the top of her head as she turned into him, cuddling against his strong body.

"I thought I'd feel more relief. Which I do. I'm glad this nightmare is finally over, it's just…"

"Your friend's still gone. I get it," he said quietly.

Yes, he did. Because he got *her*. Sighing, she closed her eyes. It was time for her to go home and move on from this madness.

* * *

Taylor was quiet as they headed up the elevator to her place, leaning back against the wall, biting on her bottom lip. She still wore the simple black dress from the funeral this morning. They'd gone back to Wyatt's condo after the call from Durnin, but Escobar and Roman's brother, who was still in town, had offered to bring most of Taylor's stuff over.

For that, Roman was grateful. Taylor's life had been basically put on hold and right now she needed to be somewhere familiar.

"They won't be too far behind us," he said quietly, referring to Escobar and Logan, mainly just to talk. He, who never made small talk. But he wanted to hear her voice, to convince himself she was okay. Today had been understandably hard on her and he just hated seeing her with puffy, red-rimmed eyes and knowing there wasn't a damn thing he could do to stop her pain.

Ease it a little, yeah, but not stop it. He'd lost enough friends overseas so he knew how hard it was to lose someone to violence. Hell, to lose someone period was difficult. And he had a feeling that things were finally starting to hit her, the reality of everything settling in.

"Yeah," she murmured, her arms crossed over her chest.

As they reached her floor, he stepped out with her, then pulled her close, turning her so that she was facing him. No one was in the hallway so he wasn't worried about lack of privacy. "I know you've got a lot to deal with right now but I'd like it if you came to Vegas for a week or two. You don't have to stay with me—but I want you to—and I think it'd be good for you to get some distance. Escobar says you're still technically not supposed to be working and I understand you want to stay busy, but it might not hurt to have some real downtime. To decompress. You witnessed violence against someone you loved. It's going to take time to heal." There was a hell of a lot more he wanted to say, but now wasn't the time. He didn't want to freaking preach at her and it was taking all his control to rein in his need to make decisions for her—because he knew that would never work with a woman like Taylor.

She blinked up at him, a hint of a smile tugging at her lips even though her eyes were so damn sad it killed him. "Thank you. I think I'm going to take you up on that offer."

"Really?"

"Don't sound so surprised. Unless you didn't, um, I mean, I don't have to stay with you. I can get a hotel room or stay with Vadim and Angel." She started to pull back but he held tight to her hips.

"I just thought I'd have to convince you more."

She shook her head and swiped at her wet eyes. "No. I need to get away from here for a bit. After today I feel so damn lost. It's hard to explain, I just . . . I can't face the thought of going back to Powers Group ever again. Maybe that's the grief talking and in a couple weeks I'll feel differently but I don't think so."

Yeah, he didn't think so either. The most selfish part of him hoped she'd take Wyatt up on his job offer. The man hadn't actually made it yet, but it was coming. He'd asked Roman if he thought Taylor would be receptive to working for him and Roman had been honest; he had no idea. But when Wyatt wanted something, he tended to go for it full throttle. Which was good because Roman wasn't letting Taylor go and if they worked in the same city, he'd get to see her a hell of a lot more than doing the long distance thing.

As they walked down the hall, Taylor linked her arm through his. "Something's been bothering me. Why would the Russians kill Neal after they'd gotten what they wanted?"

Roman had thought the same thing but they had those damn dental records. "It's possible they didn't want any ties to him if he got arrested. Maybe he had information on them. But . . . they would have just killed him sooner if that was the case. Hell, maybe he had more enemies than just the Russians." Still . . . He frowned as she pulled her key from her purse. "Can I use your phone?" Alexei had originally called Taylor from an unknown number but had later given her one so she could reach him when she was working on transferring the boat title.

"Of course." She fished out her phone and handed it to him.

He scrolled to Alexie's number. The man answered on the first ring. "Ms. Arenas, I didn't expect to hear from you again."

Roman's jaw tightened. He didn't like the other man for a myriad of reasons, but the smooth tone he was trying to use with Taylor raked against his senses. "It's Roman. We just got a call from the local PD that a mutual acquaintance is dead."

"Is there a question in there?" The man's voice was slightly mocking.

"Is Taylor safe?" Because if there was even a chance Lynch was still out there, Roman was packing her up and they were heading back to Vegas now.

A short pause. "I have no knowledge of anyone's death so if your guy is dead, it wasn't us."

"Thanks," he said before quickly hanging up. He didn't care about social niceties at the moment.

Roman placed a hand on Taylor's arm as she slid her key into the lock and twisted it. They'd called off the security watching her place after the news of

Lynch's death. But Roman didn't like the tingling in his gut that told him something was off.

"What is it?" Her brow furrowed as she looked at him.

"I don't know. Maybe nothing." Out of habit he glanced down the hall again, scanning for any potential danger, and pulled out his weapon. He handed the cell phone to her. "Move back," he whispered, wanting her away from the door.

When she took two steps away he took her arm and guided her out of the way a few doors down. He returned to her door and twisted the key in the lock to open it. Pressing his back against the wall, he reached over and twisted the handle and pushed the door open.

Gunfire immediately erupted, a hail of bullets slamming into the wall across from the door.

"Run!" he shouted, moving backward in Taylor's direction, but not turning around. He kept his weapon up, ready if the shooter exited the apartment.

His hand was steady as he moved, his actions precise. He could hear Taylor on the phone as she ran for the stairwell, calling the police, her voice shaky but her words coming through clearly.

The shooting had stopped, silence descending. "Move to the stairs," he ordered quietly. He hadn't turned enough to see her but he sensed her close behind him. She wasn't moving fast enough, damn it. He wanted her to fucking *run*.

"I'm right behind you, the police are on their way." He could hear her moving but he wasn't taking his eyes or weapon off her door even as they hurried down the hall. He didn't relish the thought of opening fire in a residential building but if the shooter revealed himself—Shit!

Lynch peeked his head out the door, his weapon raised in one hand.

Roman fired two shots in quick succession, two hits to the head. Taylor gasped behind him and he was vaguely aware of a neighbor's door opening then quickly slamming shut. He held up a hand for her to stay behind him. "Get down to the lobby using the stairs. I need to clear your place. Wait for the police." He didn't wait to see if she listened, needing to eliminate any other potential threat.

Ignoring the blood splatter and mess of Lynch's head as he passed the fallen body, Roman kicked the man's weapon away and silently swept into Taylor's place. The place was eerily quiet and thankfully it was also empty.

And he didn't feel an ounce of regret for killing Lynch. The man was a murderous bastard who, if he'd been smart, would have fled the country. But he'd thought he could come after Taylor and get away with it. Roman wasn't sure how the man had faked his dental records and he didn't much care.

The only thing that mattered was getting to Taylor and making sure she was truly safe. And he didn't plan on letting her go.

CHAPTER SEVENTEEN

Three months later

Taylor grinned at the feel of Roman's big hand sliding up her bare hip and over her stomach before grasping one of her breasts. "Just stay in bed," he murmured sleepily.

"Mm, I wish I could." Man, did she ever. "I've got to get showered and dressed though."

"You should move in with me." The statement made her freeze, then turn completely over to face him. It was early morning and streams of golden sunlight peeked through the wooden blinds of his bedroom window, bathing Roman's handsome face. And he looked wide awake, not sleepy as she'd thought. He watched her carefully, his beautiful mismatched eyes steady and intent.

Her heart caught in her throat. "Are you serious?"

"Yep." No hesitation. "Or I'll move to California. I love you, Taylor, and I can do long distance, but I don't *want* to. I want to share a home with you, to wake up to your face every damn morning."

A grin pulled at her lips as she slid her arm around him and pulled him close. "You travel for work so you wouldn't see me every morning."

He tweaked her nose, his expression lightening. "You know what I mean."

She was silent for a moment, digesting what he'd asked because it was exactly what she'd been hoping to hear from him. The last few months had been a whirlwind. She'd taken off a couple weeks after Neal had been killed and spent them with Roman in Vegas. Hugh had left her a sizeable monetary gift and some pricey real estate in his will so if she didn't want to work for a long while, she wouldn't have to. Not that she'd ever stop working. It would feel too weird to not have a purpose.

It was still hard to believe the lengths Neal had gone to in order to fake his own death. The man could have just disappeared but no, he'd needed to come after her. And he'd killed another innocent man in the process. When he'd appeared at her place, trying to kill her and Roman, she'd later wondered if he'd somehow made a cast of his teeth or something for investigators to find. She just hadn't been able to figure out how he'd faked his dental records.

It turned out he'd done something much easier than her imagination concocted. He'd switched his records with another man of similar build and age who was his dentist's patient. So when that man ended up tortured and dead, the records matched Neal's information. Since all that stuff was computerized now too he'd had to hire someone to help him hack into the dentist's system. The hacker was now in jail for that and a bunch of other fraud crimes that had nothing to do with Neal. Taylor was just glad her nightmare was truly over.

Looking at Roman, she knew the love she felt for him was visible in her eyes as she held him tight. "Well, I wasn't going to tell you until it was a done deal but it turns out I'm not heading to the airport this morning."

His eyes narrowed a fraction but he didn't respond.

"I have a meeting with Mr. Christiansen to iron out some details but he's offered me a job and barring any weird requests, I'm going to take it."

"I knew it," he muttered before leaning forward and brushing his lips over hers. He pulled back and shook his head. "The man has been acting strange lately, asking how our relationship is going."

She laughed lightly. "I wanted to surprise you after the final interview but I'll be moving here soon. I've already found someone to take over my lease and finished training my new replacement." She'd put in her notice a month ago, something Roman already knew. No matter what job path she took, she'd known she wasn't going back to Powers Group.

"Now you don't have to search for a place to live," he murmured, kissing her again, this time deeper and hungrier. He rolled on top of her, pinning her to the mattress.

She arched against his big, muscular body, wrapping her legs around him. It would be so easy to let him sink inside her, but . . . She tore her head back from his. "I can't be late to the interview."

Sighing, he laid his forehead against hers. "Fine. I'll drive you and we can have breakfast at the hotel afterward."

"Sounds good to me." She raked her fingers down his back and dug her fingers into his butt when he rolled his hips against hers, his erection a hot, solid length against her abdomen. "Maybe we have time for a quickie in the shower," she whispered. Before she'd finished the sentence, he'd shoved the covers off and was hauling her out of bed, striding for his bathroom.

Oh yeah, they'd make good use of their shower time. "I love you, Roman," she managed to get out before he pushed her up against the tiled wall of the shower.

Moaning into his mouth, she was vaguely aware of him reaching out and starting the shower before a rush of water cascaded over them. She couldn't count how many mornings they'd started out like this and she couldn't wait for countless more. Because she was in this for the long haul and she knew Roman was too—even before his brother accidentally mentioned something about an engagement ring a week ago.

The last few months had shown her that what she and Roman had was real. They'd started out under intense circumstances and yes, the attraction between them was red-hot, but more than that she liked and respected him. He'd been there for her while she dealt with her grief and everything else, had stood beside her and killed Neal to protect her.

Roman was it for her and she couldn't wait to spend the rest of her life peeling back all the layers of this amazing man. With her life back and no more threats she had the brightest sense of freedom and couldn't wait to experience everything with Roman.

Thank you for reading Dangerous Surrender. I really hope you enjoyed it and that you'll consider leaving a review at one of your favorite online retailers. It's a great way to help other readers discover new books and I appreciate all reviews.

If you would like to read more, turn the page for a sneak peek of Under His Protection. And if you don't want to miss any future releases, please feel free to join my newsletter. I only send out a newsletter for new releases or sales news. Find the signup link on my website: http://www.katiereus.com

UNDER HIS PROTECTION
Red Stone Security Series
Copyright © 2014 Katie Reus

Julieta Mederos looked up from her computer screen as the bell above her shop door jingled. She inwardly cringed. She thought she'd locked the door. It was ten minutes until closing but as the owner of Julieta's Silk and Lace she could make executive decisions. And it was Friday night, she was starving, and the employee she'd had scheduled to close this evening had called in sick. Again.

Since no one else had been able to come in, she'd been stuck covering. *Again.* She hated to let anyone go, but tomorrow morning she was making the call.

Shoving those thoughts away she smiled at the beautiful couple entering. "Hi, please feel free to shop around and let me know if you have any questions about anything."

The woman was tall, slender and wearing a long, bright print Bohemian-style dress with simple gold sandals. She was truly stunning, the kind of woman Julieta wouldn't be surprised to see gracing the cover of a magazine. She smiled back, her expression tentative. "I saw the hours on your door, are you sure you're still open?" When she fingered the strap of her purse, the giant diamond on her left hand, ring finger glinted under the colorful track lighting.

Julieta nodded, already liking the woman from that one thoughtful question. "I'm Julieta so I can stay open as late as you'd like." She flicked a glance to the tall, blond man standing next to her. He looked like a sexy Viking god. Well, a sexy, angry one. He was practically glaring at her. *Okay then.*

Maybe Julieta's discomfort showed on her face because the woman nudged the male in the sharp black suit next to her. "I'm going to shop and my friend here is going to sit right over there." There was an edge to her voice as the woman pointed to a plush couch next to a glass-cased display of discreet sex toys.

Practically growling, the man went to stand next to the couch, turning his body so that he had a view of the front door and the rest of the shop. As Julieta watched him she realized just how huge he was. Most people were taller than her anyway, but with broad shoulders and a muscular body even a suit couldn't hide, a sliver of anxiety threaded through her veins. She'd never been robbed before, but she wasn't stupid enough to think it couldn't happen to her.

Julieta sold high-end lingerie, but she also sold affordable, quality fashion jewelry and sex toys. Some days it amazed her how many toys she sold. Remaining where she was, she placed her hand on the silent alarm button under the display case. "Just let me know if you need help." She made it a point not to crowd her customers unless it was clear they needed assistance and she wanted to keep some distance between herself and the big man in case he tried anything.

"I actually do need help. My friend Elizabeth Porter recommended this place to me," the woman said as she strode farther into the shop, her gold bangles jangling around her wrist noisily.

"Lizzy?"

Smiling widely, the woman nodded. "Yes. We're new friends actually. I just moved to Miami a month ago and my fiancé works for the same company Lizzy and her husband do."

Julieta let her hand drop from hovering over the silent alarm. That explained the man's military-style stance as if he was guarding or casing the place. She tilted her head to the man standing stiffly in the front of her store. "He's with Red Stone too?"

She nodded. "Yes, but he's not my fiancé. That's Ivan Mitchell. He's my personal guard."

Julieta started to raise her eyebrows then caught herself. "Well I'm more than happy to help a friend of Lizzy's. Our mothers go way back and I've known Lizzy since we were kids."

The woman smiled. "That's what she said. She said she's a couple years younger than you and used to follow you around like a puppy dog whenever your parents got together."

At that, Julieta let out a sharp bark of laughter and rounded the counter, all anxiety about the sexy Ivan dissipating. "I don't know about that, but she was quite attentive."

The woman's shoulders relaxed slightly, her sun-kissed arms a nice bronze. "I'm Mina."

"Nice to meet you. You can call me Jules. Why don't you tell me what I can help you with?"

The woman flicked a glance to the front of the store. Julieta followed her line of sight to see the sexy Viking watching them intently again. She squirmed under his glare. It was like he expected her to pull out a weapon at any moment.

Not liking the way he watched her, she turned back to Mina. The tall woman bent slightly, as if wanting to tell her a secret. "I didn't want to bring him but he insisted on coming inside." She let out an annoyed sigh before continuing. "Lizzy said you sold the best lingerie in town and that you sold fun . . . toys," she said in a whisper. Her cheeks tinged crimson and Julieta bit back a smile.

It was always fun to introduce women to their first sex toys. Sadly for her, toys had been her only form of companionship the last three years. Gah, she couldn't even think about that. Nodding, she said, "Are you looking for solo toys or something you can use with your fiancé? Maybe as a surprise for him?" She was just guessing but she'd gotten good at reading her customers the past couple years.

"Definitely with him. And yes, it's a surprise."

"If we can move your scary bodyguard away from the case up front, I think I've got a few things that might interest you. If you decide you like something, I can have it delivered or you can take it with you today—discreetly packaged. And if you don't find anything you like, I have a catalogue you can check out too."

Relief bled into Mina's dark green eyes. "My fiancé, Alex, is coming back tonight from an out of town trip so I'm sure I'll find something."

Julieta nodded and forced herself to ignore the intent stare from the blond-haired, blue-eyed god standing up front as she led Mina to the display case. She'd met enough judgmental men to last a lifetime, thank you very much. Maybe he didn't like the fact that she sold sex toys. Heaven forbid women please themselves on their own. Whatever his problem was, she didn't give a crap. He wasn't her customer and she didn't have time to worry about it.

ACKNOWLEDGMENTS

A great big thank you to my family for putting up with my hectic schedule. Your patience is so appreciated! I'm often saying thanks to the usual crowd and this time is no different. Thank you to Kari Walker for her help getting this book just right, Joan Turner for copy editing, Jaycee with Sweet 'N Spicy Designs for her wonderful cover, and Amy with Author E.M.S. for always fitting me into her schedule. To my readers, thank you for reading this series. I hope you enjoyed Roman's story! As always, I'm so thankful to God for being a continuing presence in my life.

COMPLETE BOOKLIST

Red Stone Security Series
No One to Trust
Danger Next Door
Fatal Deception
Miami, Mistletoe & Murder
His to Protect
Breaking Her Rules
Protecting His Witness
Sinful Seduction
Under His Protection

The Serafina: Sin City Series
First Surrender
Sensual Surrender
Sweetest Surrender
Dangerous Surrender

Deadly Ops Series
Targeted
Bound to Danger

Non-series Romantic Suspense
Running From the Past

Everything to Lose
Dangerous Deception
Dangerous Secrets
Killer Secrets
Deadly Obsession
Danger in Paradise
His Secret Past

Paranormal Romance
Destined Mate
Protector's Mate
A Jaguar's Kiss
Tempting the Jaguar
Enemy Mine
Heart of the Jaguar

Moon Shifter Series
Alpha Instinct
Lover's Instinct (novella)
Primal Possession
Mating Instinct
His Untamed Desire (novella)
Avenger's Heat
Hunter Reborn

Darkness Series
Darkness Awakened
Taste of Darkness

ABOUT THE AUTHOR

Katie Reus is the *New York Times* and *USA Today* bestselling author of the Red Stone Security series, the Moon Shifter series and the Deadly Ops series. She fell in love with romance at a young age thanks to books she pilfered from her mom's stash. Years later she loves reading romance almost as much as she loves writing it.

However, she didn't always know she wanted to be a writer. After changing majors many times, she finally graduated summa cum laude with a degree in psychology. Not long after that she discovered a new love. Writing. She now spends her days writing dark paranormal romance and sexy romantic suspense. For more information on Katie please visit her website: www.katiereus.com. Also find her on twitter @katiereus or visit her on facebook at: www.facebook.com/katiereusauthor.

Made in the USA
Lexington, KY
28 October 2016